Lily Quench

and the Lighthouse of Skellig Mor

Lily Quench

and the Lighthouse of Skellig Mor

NATALIE JANE PRIOR

Illustrations by Janine Dawson

PUFFIN BOOKS

For Elizabeth

PUFFIN BOOKS
Published by Penguin Group
Penguin Young Readers Group,
345 Hudson Street, New York, New York 10014, U.S.A.
Penguin Books Ltd, 80 Strand, London WC2R ORL, England
Penguin Books Australia Ltd, 250 Camberwell Road, Camberwell, Victoria 3124, Australia
Penguin Books Canada Ltd, 10 Alcorn Avenue, Toronto, Ontario, Canada M4V 3B2
Penguin Books (N.Z.) Ltd, 182-190 Wairau Road, Auckland 10, New Zealand

First published in Australia and New Zealand by Hodder Headline Australia Pty Limited
(A member of the Hodder Headline Group),
Level 22, 201 Kent Street, Sydney NSW 2000, 2003
Published by Puffin Books, a division of Penguin Young Readers Group, 2004

1   3   5   7   9   10   8   6   4   2

LIBRARY OF CONGRESS CATALOGING-IN-PUBLICATION DATA

Prior, Natalie Jane, 1963-
Lily Quench and the lighthouse of Skellig Mor / Natalie Jane Prior ; illustrations by Janine Dawson.
p. cm.
Summary: In their ongoing quest to find a way to close the Eye Stones
and secure the land of Ashby from time-traveling invaders, Lily Quench and her
friend Dragon Queen visit a group of mysterious islands where they befriend a
lighthouse keeper and find a clue in a book with magical properties.
ISBN 0-14-240059-9 (pbk.)
[1. Books and reading—Fiction. 2. Dragons—Fiction.
3. Islands—Fiction. 4. Fantasy.] I. Dawson, Janine, ill. II. Title.
PZ7.P9373Ll 2004 [Fic]—dc22 2003068976

Printed in the United States of America

Sea Dragon Nursery

The

Great

Weavers House

Moonflower orchards

Southern

Drihtan's Palace & undersea tunnel

Library

Skellig Lir

Archipelago

Whirlpool

Queen Dragon's Rock

The Cauldron

Lighthouse

beach

Skellig Mor

The first Island Lily flies over

chapter one
Flight to the South

High above the Southern Ocean, where the sea dragons play and the whales make their winter home, and lonely islands that the outside world has scarcely heard of cluster, a small red speck flew steadily southward. It soared silently through the clouds, with hardly a flap of its enormous wings to carry it onward. On a rocky island with a tall tower, a girl looked up hopefully as its shadow passed overhead, but the bright pale sunlight dazzled her eyes, and she could not make out exactly what it was.

Only the sea dragons, plunging and undulating through the chilly seas, were able to tell it was a dragon. It was not one of their own kind, for sea dragons are flightless and almost colorless out of water; they take their hues from the ocean, blue and green on sunlit days, and cloudy gray in stormy weather. This dragon was red and of royal aspect, with wings that were terrifying in their extent. The keen eyes of the sea dragons could also discern a small human figure seated on the dragon's head. It was a girl with long hair and a winged helmet flashing silver in the sunlight. She wore red boots and a leather flying jacket, and behind her a curious cloak streamed and shimmered like a tongue of fire in the thin air.

Slowly at first, then more rapidly, the great red dragon started coming down through the clouds. This time the girl on the island saw it in the distance and realized what it was. An idea started forming in her head, a wild idea that saw her flying from her life of misery to escape and freedom. She opened her mouth and flung up her arms to call the dragon back. But even if her puny yells could have been heard over the roar of the ocean, the dragon was already out of earshot.

Like everybody else, it had not even noticed she was there.

Coming down from the clouds, Lily Quench dug her feet into the scales on Queen Dragon's head and clung with all her might to the luggage harness. They were nearing the end of a long, wearisome journey, flying over jungles and the wastelands of the lost Southern Continent, and traveling across more ocean than Lily had ever realized existed. Now, below them was the beginning of the great Southern Archipelago, the cluster of islands that hung off the southern tip of the world, a mysterious and, some said, magical destination. It was also the location of the great Library of Skellig Lir, where Lily hoped to find magical books that would help her secure her homeland of Ashby against an invasion of enemies from the past.

Once, an unknown evil had built magical doorways through time that allowed anyone who knew how to use them to travel wherever and whenever they wished. For centuries, no one had remembered the Eye Stones existed. Now they had been rediscovered, and an army was gathering in the past to come and reconquer Ashby for Gordon, the Black Count, whose father had ruled Ashby in misery for many years. The way through from the past had to be closed off before that could happen. But no one in Ashby knew how to do that, and so King Lionel and Queen Evangeline had sent Lily and Queen Dragon on a quest to find the answer with only the faint scent of magic on the southern trade winds to guide them.

At times Lily had doubted they would ever find what they were looking for. Then, an hour ago, Queen Dragon had flown over the first teardrop-shaped island, and now whole clutches of them lay stretched out below. Some islands were little more than rocks poking treacherously up out of the sea. Others were quite big and glowed like jewels in the afternoon sunlight, with snow-capped mountains and pine woods marching down to their rocky shores. The sea was a clearer color, as if shallower and cleaner, and here and there Lily saw silvery gray shapes moving with the waves. From time to time a hump appeared above the surface, or a forked tail rose and fell, sending up a great splash of water. Lily bent down to shout into the little hole that was Queen Dragon's ear.

"Look, Queen Dragon! Sea monsters!"

"Not exactly, Lily," Queen Dragon replied. "They're actually sea dragons. Not my kind of dragon, but distant relations. I've been watching them for a while. I've never seen so many in one place before."

"I wonder what they're doing?" Lily reached for the telescope she carried in a satchel slung over her shoulder and trained it on the water. Now she could see that there were many more sea dragons than she had realized. Swarms of them were swimming swiftly just under the surface of the water. They seemed to be congregating in a strait between two islands that were coming up on the right.

"It's very strange, isn't it?" said Queen Dragon. She paused. "Of course, it's none of our business, but it is rather interesting. Shall we go down for a closer look?"

She tucked in her wings and started descending even more steeply toward the ocean. As they leveled out, Lily saw that the sea dragons were swimming slowly around and around a central point. All of them were going in the same direction and at the same speed, as if they were caught up in some monstrous water ballet. Lily could see nothing on the surface to explain why they were so excited and wondered if they were circling something that lay underwater.

It reminded Lily of the shoals of fish that sometimes swam past her home on the Island of Skansey. The fish obviously knew where they were going, even if nobody else did. But the fish were tiny, the size of Lily's forefinger, while each sea dragon was as long as a small passenger train. The sight of their scaly, sinuous bodies snaking through the sea was so breathtaking that it was several moments before Lily noticed something else, which she had missed before. A small black and red boat was wallowing in the waves where the sea dragons congregated, in obvious danger of being swamped.

"There's a boat! The sea dragons are hassling it, Queen Dragon. I think it's going to sink!" Lily trained her telescope on the deck and saw six or eight terrified people clinging to the sides and throwing gaffs, barrels, anything they could lay their hands on at the creatures in the water. One man aimed a harpoon at a sea dragon that was approaching too closely; another tried vainly to steer the vessel out of danger. Two women were struggling to inflate a portable life raft. As Lily watched, the boat hit a wave side-on, and both women were tipped, screaming, into the sea.

Queen Dragon banked and started flying toward the boat. The women were bobbing about in their yellow life jackets, but the waves had carried them away from the boat, and it was too rough for them to swim. Queen Dragon swooped over their heads, but the sight of her only made them scream more hysterically than ever. The harpooner fired a useless missile into the sky. It bounced off Queen Dragon's side and fell into the sea.

"We're trying to *help* you!" Lily shouted, but nobody could hear a word she said. "Queen Dragon—what can we do? If we leave them, they'll drown, or the sea dragons will eat them!"

"I can't land on the water, Lily," replied Queen

Dragon. "And, in any case, I think it's already too late. Look." She wheeled around, and Lily saw one of the sea dragons bearing down on the women in the life jackets.

"Oh, no!"

The harpooner fired again, this time straight between the creature's eyes, but the sea dragon did not appear to be hurt, or even dented. Instead, with a horrible cry that sounded like a wave trapped in the back of its throat, it opened its jaws and rushed toward the boat.

The sailors either ran for cover or hit the deck. An enormous wash of water hit the boat's side and swamped the decks. The sea dragon's jaws opened wider than Lily could have believed possible. It grasped the entire front of the boat and snapped it off in its mouth as if it were made of gingerbread.

The boat started to founder and break up. The sailors jumped or pitched headlong into the water. Briefly the sea dragon sank beneath the waves. Then, with a cry like an eruption, its great head burst up through the waves, picking up the entire boat and tossing it aside like a toy.

Lily screamed. The wrecked boat disappeared,

gurgling horribly down into the depths, and the air was filled with the dreadful cries of drowning people.

"Help!" Lily cried. "Somebody help us!" She looked around wildly for some sign of another boat, or even inhabitants on the nearest islands, but there was nothing there. And then the most incredible thing happened.

The breeze, which had been blowing stiffly, suddenly dropped. The air filled with a strong perfume, like roses, gardenias, hyacinths, and every other sweetly smelling flower Lily knew rolled into one. A shadow passed over Lily's head, and she looked up and gasped. Giant, pearly pink-tinged bubbles came drifting down out of the sky, like thistledown from a dandelion clock.

"What—" Lily gaped, and even Queen Dragon looked astonished. The bubbles sailed down and bounced lightly across the waves, each one landing by a drowning sailor and picking him or her up. Then they rose from the surface of the water and floated away. As one flew close by her, Lily saw one of the women in the yellow life jackets and caught a glimpse of her disbelieving face pressed up against the bubble wall.

"Queen Dragon, what's happening?"

"I don't know, but it feels like magic to me," Queen Dragon began. Suddenly something loomed above her, and she squawked and faltered in mid–wing stroke. Lily looked up, and almost fell from her perch. A huge pink object was flying down toward her and was about to collide with her head.

chapter two

In the Court of the Drihtan

"Lily! Lily! Oh my, what's happening?" Queen Dragon felt something brushing against her head. She looked up and saw an enormous bubble floating away with Lily inside it. Around her, other bubbles containing rescued sailors were rising from the surface of the ocean. Queen Dragon thought she saw Lily's fists banging against the walls of her bubble, and heard her shouting in vain for help. But the thing was traveling so swiftly it was impossible to be sure.

One giant wingtip raked the surface of the ocean as Queen Dragon banked over the shipwreck and started climbing after the bubble. But the sheer number of bubbles confused her, and, by the time her laboring wing strokes had carried her back to the level of the clouds, the one with Lily in it had almost disappeared. Queen Dragon caught a glimpse of Lily's bubble floating over a mountain on a distant island. After that it grew so small that even her keen dragon eyesight could no longer distinguish it.

"Oh, rats, rats, *rats!*" Queen Dragon cried. She turned back and circled the area distractedly, speaking out loud in the dragon language she had learned as a young hatchling and that she now used only to herself. "Lily! *Lily!* What do I do now? Why do these things always happen to me? Hey, you—down there! You know this is all your fault, don't you?"

The sea dragons did not even bother to look

up. With a heavy heart, Queen Dragon wheeled around and flapped off in search of an island where she could sit and ponder what on earth she was going to do next.

Inside the bubble, Lily watched the bright red blotch that was Queen Dragon grow swiftly smaller, then disappear. She was not entirely sure what was happening, and it was hard not to panic. She had no idea where she was being taken. Clearly the bubble had snatched her from Queen Dragon's head, and, though it was true the bubbles *had* rescued the drowning sailors, there was no guarantee that its ultimate intentions were going to be friendly.

For a moment Lily closed her eyes. She pictured Queen Dragon, who had rescued her so many times before, and told herself that she would surely follow her. Then she thought of the long line of Quenches who had gone before her, of her forebears Mad Brian and Matilda the Drakescourge, and her grandmother Old Ursula, the bravest person Lily had ever known. These thoughts did something to restore her courage. When she opened her eyes again, she was calm enough to try to work out what she should do next.

The bubble was flying south at a tremendous speed, apparently carrying her farther into the archipelago. It was hard to see much through its rounded walls at all, and, when Lily touched them, the sides sprang back against her fingertips. Lily checked the satchel containing her telescope, drink bottle, and uneaten provisions, and her sword in its scabbard strapped to her belt. Everything was still there, but nothing seemed immediately useful. All she could do was pop or deflate the bubble, and she had no intention of doing that.

"Where are you taking me?" she asked aloud. But the bubble was obviously not clever enough to answer, and after a few more questions Lily gave up. She sat down, feeling a bit like a small human pebble on the bottom of a giant goldfish bowl, and ate some dried fruit and drank some water to pass the time.

At last the bubble started going down. It crossed the coast of an island and skimmed over fields of long, waving grass. Lily glimpsed buildings, trees, and paved roads. The bubble flew up over a high wall, down a tree-lined avenue, and through a tall, pillared gateway. With a little bounce it landed on hard pavement. Then, with a gentle popping sensation that took Lily by surprise, it was gone.

Lily looked up. She was sitting cross-legged and alone in the middle of a walled courtyard. Overhead were fluffy white clouds, blue sky, and two swallows winging their way to a mud nest on one of the walls. There were no people anywhere to be seen, but somewhere beyond the walls she could hear women singing a gentle repetitive song that somehow lifted her spirits. A beautiful perfume spiced the air. It seemed to be coming from the trees that were growing up along the walls of the courtyard; they were covered with blowzy pink and mauve blossoms that Lily had never seen before in any garden. Birds chirped. In the distance she could hear the sound of waves breaking on the shore.

Lily stood up. She no longer felt afraid. It was simply impossible to believe anyone could hurt her in such a lovely place. Beneath her feet, gleaming blue and green tiles stretched away to a portico, set with a pair of gilded doors. The blue parts of the pavement were flecked with tiny white lines, like the tops of waves, and painted in among them were the shadowy forms of sea dragons. Here and there green sections of tile represented islands. It was a map of the archipelago. When Lily stood still, she almost thought she could hear the sounds of the sea coming up from the tiny waves.

Step by step, she began exploring the map. Here were gray shoals of rock with waves crashing treacherously upon them, and here a flock of seabirds wheeled around a lonely crag sticking up from the ocean. But it was the hundreds of islands that really interested Lily. Most were simply green and bare, but a few had houses on them, and several were covered with tiny representations of flowering trees. In the very center of the courtyard was an island made from what looked like pure gold. It was shaped a little like a horseshoe, with a second, smaller island in the middle of the U-shape. The big island bristled with gardens and miniature buildings, but the small one contained only one round building with columns and a crystal cupola.

Suddenly, the sun came out from behind a cloud. The golden island on the pavement reflected the light so that Lily's eyes were unexpectedly dazzled. She blinked and, through the glare, saw the doors beneath the portico open. A woman emerged and walked across the courtyard toward her. She was dressed in a flowing blue gown with a gold brocade cloak, but it was not this that made Lily gasp aloud with astonishment. For the woman was unlike anyone Lily had ever seen or even heard of. She had pale, golden skin, silver hair, and four arms.

"Good afternoon, Lily Quench," the woman said.

Lily belatedly remembered her manners and removed her helmet. She made a low curtsy.

"Good afternoon, ma'am."

The woman smiled. "Welcome to Skellig Lir, Lily," she said. "I am sorry if your journey here alarmed you. I am Romina, a servant of the Drihtan who rules these islands. It was he who ordered the moon bubbles to rescue the sailors and bring you to the palace. Don't worry. The sailors are on their way home as we speak. We have a responsibility to look after all those who enter our territory, even thieves and trespassers."

"Thieves and trespassers!" Lily's heart sank at the words, but Romina reassuringly shook her head.

"Don't worry," she said. "We know you and your dragon friend mean us no harm. But the sailors from that boat are different. Every year when the moon roses are in flower, intruders come to the archipelago hoping to steal them. Luckily the sea dragons keep watch for us, and they rarely get farther than the Outer Islands."

"Is Queen Dragon safe?" asked Lily anxiously. "Why didn't you bring her here, too?"

"I'm afraid the moon bubbles have their limits," replied Romina, with a laugh. "Queen Dragon is far too big to travel in one. But, I assure you, she is perfectly safe, and you will rejoin her in due course. Come with me, and I will take you to the Drihtan. He will be able to answer all your questions."

The portico doors opened at the lift of her hand. Together, she and Lily passed into a cool, dim corridor. It had a golden ceiling with walls that gleamed like mother-of-pearl, and it curled around itself like the inside of a huge shell. When they had almost reached the middle of the shell, they stopped at a door made of what looked like solid gold. Romina rapped once on a knocker shaped like a sea dragon and ushered Lily inside.

Inside the room a man was seated on a throne. He was not particularly old, but his face was wise, and across his lap lay a staff made out of a whitish wood that he held with his four golden hands. Around the dais where he sat were marvelous hangings made of cloth of gold and a fabulous fabric that seemed to shimmer like a flame: first red, then magenta, then purple. It looked oddly familiar. Lily glanced down at her fireproof cape and gave an involuntary gasp.

"Yes," said the Drihtan in an amused voice. "Your cape was made here on Skellig Lir, Lily. I see it is rather worn and in need of repair. You have obviously been through many adventures with it. Please, be seated, and welcome."

He waved one of his hands, and a servant brought Lily a carved chair. It bristled with sea dragons, shells, and breaking waves, but, when Lily sat down, the uncomfortable-looking carvings seemed to move and settle around her, as if the wood were somehow still alive. As soon as she was settled, the Drihtan turned once more to his servant. The man came forward, this time carrying a golden bowl full of what looked like very clear water.

The Drihtan pulled back a sleeve and plunged a hand into the water. To Lily's amazement, he brought out a book. Its cover glowed the color of sapphires and, when he held it out to her, the shimmering water ran into tiny droplets that broke and glistened on his skin.

Lily leaned forward in her chair and hesitantly took the book. As it passed into her hands she thought she saw a little flash, and felt a tingle of something that was neither excitement nor electricity, but something in between. Then she gave a loud cry and almost dropped it.

The picture on the cover was of herself.

chapter three
The Library of Skellig Lir

In the middle of the ocean, Queen Dragon sat weeping on a rock. Most humans would have called it a small island, but Queen Dragon was so big she took up most of it, and, to her, it was a rock. She was, in truth, extremely tired and depressed. Her hot dragon tears fell into the sea and sent up drifts of steam. She had absolutely no idea what she was going to do.

Longingly, Queen Dragon thought of her volcano, especially the great hoard of metal she kept there. She had made a frugal supper of the

metal mast of the wrecked boat, which she had
been lucky enough to find floating on the surface
of the water, but she had not eaten properly for
over a week, and hunger made her feel only
worse about Lily's disappearance. Queen Dragon
knew that Lily was an intrepid adventurer who
had looked after herself in many terrible
situations. But she was still very small and young,
and, in her heart, Queen Dragon thought of her
as a hatchling who had to be constantly guided
and watched over.

Compared to dragons, humans were like
flowers that opened for a day and then were
gone. It was hard sometimes for Queen Dragon
to have to remind herself that Lily really was
human, and that her little life span, like all human
life spans, would very quickly flash by. Lily could
be as brave as a dragon, and she often acted like
one, too. But nothing could turn Lily into a real
dragon, and now that she had been stolen away
by the bubble there was no saying what might
happen to her.

Queen Dragon sat up and spread her enormous
wings. "Lily!" she shouted at the top of her voice.
"Lily, can you hear me?"

Suddenly a sharp gust of wind eddied across the surface of the ocean. It caught Queen Dragon under her wings and nearly tipped her off the rock. Queen Dragon squawked and righted herself with difficulty. As another gust of wind rattled past, she looked up and saw a dark swath of cloud on the northern horizon rolling ominously toward her.

"Lily! Lily! *Lily!*"

In the Drihtan's throne room Lily stood staring at the book in her hands.

"That's me!" she stammered. "Why—what am I doing on the cover of a book?"

"You're there because it is a book about you," said the Drihtan. His face was amused. "It is the story of your first encounter with Queen Dragon, Lily. And this—" he produced a purple book "—is the story of your quest to discover the blue lily in the snows of the Black Mountains. It tells of the death of the Black Count and your meeting with his son, Gordon. In the next volume we read how Gordon fled into the past, and how you followed him and discovered the long-lost Treasure of Mote Ely." He smiled. "Shall I read you a few pages from the last chapter? 'Then the cellar wall was breached, and in the cave beyond were wonderful things, a treasure richer and more beautiful than anything Lily could have imagined, a treasure that made her and Lionel and Evangeline dance and weep with joy. For what was there was enough to make Ashby the richest kingdom east of the Black Mountains. After long years of poverty and hardship, Ashby Water and its castle could be rebuilt.'"

"It's true we've had many bad times in Ashby," said Lily slowly. "And they haven't finished yet. As long as the Eye Stones remain open, there's always a chance that Gordon will come back from the past with his army. Our king, Lionel, sent me here because he hoped that an answer to our problem would be found in your magical library."

"As to that, I cannot say," said the Drihtan. "But you have my permission to ask the librarian. Follow me. I will take you to her."

He stood up and beckoned Lily to stand close beside him. Then he clapped his hands, and the whole dais began to sink down slowly through the floor. It was a little like being in an elevator with no walls, ceilings, or shaft. When they had sunk through nothing into a room about the same size as the throne room, the dais stopped. Lily and the Drihtan stepped off, and it rose again silently, without ropes or pulleys, into the ceiling far above.

The room was softly lit and filled with doors. There must have been a dozen or more of them, all bewilderingly similar, but the Drihtan selected one without hesitation and unlocked it with a small gold key. He led Lily through it and down a spiral staircase. Golden censers hung from hooks in its walls and burned with a clean, scented light. At the bottom was another door, inlaid with mother-of-pearl. This time the Drihtan handed the key to Lily.

"Turn it in the lock and see if it will let you through," he said.

Lily took the key. It was unexpectedly heavy, with an elaborately carved shank and a loop at the end that was studded with emeralds. She slipped it into the lock and turned it. The lock clicked, and the door swung open.

"You pass the first test," said the Drihtan softly.

"This door would never have let you pass if your intentions were evil. There will be another test when we reach the library. Follow me."

He stepped through the door. After a few steps the glow from the staircase behind them was replaced by a greenish light. To her astonishment, Lily realized they were under the sea. It was a bit like being inside a fish tank without getting wet. Above them the waves washed and swam over a crystal roof, and she could see fish, darting in shoals or flicking lazily past, as well as the occasional jellyfish or sea snake. At last they reached the end of the tunnel. A door was set there, and, beyond it, another staircase led up to a small round room.

"We are now in the anteroom to the Library of Skellig Lir," the Drihtan said. He indicated a bell on a tripod. "Ring the bell, Lily. The librarian will decide whether you may go any farther."

Lily took hold of the cord that hung from the bell and shook it. At once the bell sounded, so loud and clear that it made her jump, for it was as if several perfectly tuned bells were ringing at once. The sound hung in the air, then slowly faded. A round door opened on the opposite side of the room, and a woman came out.

Lily immediately went down on her knees. She was not sure why, but the Drihtan had done the same, and something about the librarian seemed to call for it. Unlike the other people she had met on Skellig Lir, she seemed at first glance to be an ordinary human woman. She was small, with a long brown braid hanging over one shoulder and a calm, unlined face. When the librarian moved, the air seemed to sigh and tremble around her, like the wind in the great grasslands that surrounded the Singing Wood. When she spoke, it was in a clear voice like the bell that had summoned her.

"It is true that the library here contains what you seek, Lily Quench. But what do you want? What kind of magic do you expect to find?"

"Well, something to close off the Eye Stones." Lily was confused. "I thought you might have a spell, or a charm we could borrow. I want—"

But she did not get a chance to finish her sentence. The library door had already slammed shut.

"I am sorry," said the Drihtan as they walked back under the sea. "I suspected this would happen, but of course I could say nothing until you had spoken to the librarian yourself."

"But what did I do to upset her?" asked Lily despairingly. "I passed the first test, so she knows I mean well. What should I have said?"

"I cannot tell you that," said the Drihtan. "You must find out for yourself, and, when you know the answer, you will be permitted to come back and ask again. I can, however, tell you this much, Lily. Many centuries ago a party of human magicians came to these islands. They traveled in iron cauldrons and used spells to ward off the sea dragons. Despite all this we welcomed them and allowed them into the library. But they tricked us. They stole one of the magical books and damaged the library beyond repair. After that, we set up the tests, and the librarian has rarely ever admitted Outsiders. I am sorry your journey has been in vain."

Lily nodded. She was close to tears, but there

seemed to be nothing she could do or say to change things. They entered the room with the doors, and the Drihtan summoned the dais down from the throne room with a click of his staff against the flagstones. They rode back up in silence.

Romina was waiting for them in the throne room. Lily noticed it seemed to have grown dark somehow, though all the lamps were lit. She looked up and saw that the golden ceiling had turned as transparent as glass. In their absence the sky had darkened. The clouds were black, like a gigantic bruise on the face of the heavens, and a huge storm seemed to be blowing up from the north.

Romina came anxiously forward. "Lord Drihtan, there is terrible news from the Outer Islands. Ariane has disappeared from Skellig Mor again! There are more sea dragons in the straits than I have ever seen, and a storm is running straight for Skellig Lir. Look at the clouds! If we don't find Ariane soon, there's no telling how long it will last!"

"Queen Dragon!" Lily exclaimed. "She's still out there, on the ocean!"

Romina and the Drihtan turned as if they had forgotten all about her.

"I fear the storm has already hit the Outer Islands, Lily," said the Drihtan. "But come with us quickly. We should be able to tell whether Queen Dragon is safe by looking at the map."

Outside in the courtyard where Lily had arrived, everything had changed. Strong winds were already ripping at the trees on the walls, sending up flurries of purple petals. A huge spatter of cold raindrops fell on Lily's upturned face as she left the shelter of the portico. When she looked at the tiles on the pavement, she saw that they had turned a hideous gray and white, like waves churning in a tempest.

Romina and the Drihtan paced the pavement.

"Can you see Ariane?" Romina asked.

"No. But there must be two or three hundred sea dragons in the Outer Islands." The Drihtan pointed with his staff. Lily looked and saw to her amazement that the sea was thick with them, like maggots writhing on a piece of meat. Then she saw something else that made her heart turn over. It was a small—a very small—red representation of a winged dragon on one of the tiniest islands in the grouping, a gray speck that was no more than a rock in the middle of an angry sea.

"Queen Dragon!"

"That island is about to go under," said Romina. "The storms do not happen often, but when they come, they are fierce and unexpected. Your friend is in terrible danger."

"Can't she fly to another island?"

"The winds will be too strong. They would rip her wings to pieces in less than a minute."

Lily stared helplessly at the pavement. As she watched, a couple of nearby islands disappeared completely under the tossing waves. Then, before her horrified eyes, the red dot that was Queen Dragon fluttered like an autumn leaf, blinked, and disappeared.

chapter four
Storms at Sea

"No!" screamed Lily. "Queen Dragon! No!" Lightning struck and a huge roll of thunder rattled the heavens. Then the rain came in earnest, bucketing out of the sky and drenching everything. Romina tried to grab Lily's arm, but she threw it off.

"Lily! Come inside!"

"We can't leave her! You've got to take me back!"

"She's gone, Lily. She must have been washed away. I'm sorry, there's nothing we can do."

"No!" Lily slipped from Romina's grasp and ran wildly across the courtyard. The outer doors swung open at her touch. She dashed through the avenue of trees into open grassland, running as fast as she could, not knowing where she was headed or even why. The flowing grass whipped at her skirts, and the rain soaked her hair and clothes. It was falling so heavily that she could hardly see where she was going. Behind her she could just hear Romina's voice, shouting a warning.

"Come back, Lily! Come back, it's dangerous!"

"No!" The wind was so strong Lily could hardly stand without being blown over. She saw bits of fences, plants, even a helpless chicken driven along by the blast. Pink blossoms from the trees filled the air like a snowstorm. The clouds were a horrible combination of green and black and gray, and, when lightning shot through them, the thunder followed so quickly it almost pierced her eardrums.

Suddenly, there was a tremendous rending sound, and a giant branch ripped off a nearby tree and spun across her path. Lily lost her balance and skidded over. She started scrambling to her feet and, behind her, heard a creak as if the world were being split in two. Lily looked up and saw the tree looming above her. There was a roar and a rattle of branches, and then the entire tree came crashing down on top of her.

"*Lily! Lily!*" Queen Dragon bellowed. "*Somebody! Anybody! Help me!*"

A huge wave, higher than a house, came smashing down on the little rock where Queen Dragon was perched. For the umpteenth time, she slipped and righted herself, almost falling into the sea. Several times she had tried to fly away, and several times the wind had nearly ripped her wings off. She was sick, terrified, and almost unable to think from the sound and force of the water beating against her rock.

The sea was alive with waterspouts. The clouds sparked with lightning, and the thunder was like an army of diabolical kettledrums bearing down upon her. If Queen Dragon had not already been so tired it would not have been so bad. But she was physically exhausted, and the constant drenching was making her perilously cold. Her muscles were stiff, and it was becoming hard to move, harder still to cling on to the rock. She felt as if the fires inside her were almost out. The sound of her voice calling for help was lost in the tempest, but there was no other hope of rescue, and so she kept on shouting forlornly for someone to come to her.

"Help! Help! *Help!*"

"Hold on!" called a little voice. "I'm coming!"

Queen Dragon blinked. She could hardly believe she had heard it, but it had sounded human. After a moment she decided she must have imagined it: no human could possibly shout loud enough to be heard over the storm's fury. But the voice sounded again, as if it were speaking right inside her head, and this time there was no mistaking what it said.

"Hold on!"

Queen Dragon squinted through the driving rain. For a moment she caught a glimpse, but only a glimpse, of a small round boat like an iron cauldron. It appeared to be making its way toward her, and there was a girl sitting inside it. The cauldron disappeared into the trough of a wave, and Queen Dragon thought it had gone, but then it appeared again on the crest, spinning around like an out-of-control toy top. The cauldron's shape was such that Queen Dragon could see only the girl's head, with a round helmet on it like a small cooking pot, and what looked like a trident in her hand. The boat skimmed and bounced on the huge waves, but there was a stillness that surrounded it, a sphere of calm that made it somehow possible for it to stay afloat. Queen Dragon narrowed her yellow, reptile eyes. After four thousand years of hard-earned experience, she knew bad magic when she saw it.

At length, the little boat made it to the island. The sphere of calm surrounding it stretched over the rock and Queen Dragon sitting upon it. As it passed over her body, the storm around her seemed to stop, and she was suddenly warm again. It was the strangest sensation, a bit like suddenly getting off the fastest fairground ride in the world and standing on solid ground. Queen Dragon was not sure what to make of it.

"Who are you?" she asked. Her voice boomed unexpectedly, as if bouncing off the walls of a very small room. The girl winced and clapped two hands over her ears.

"Ouch! Do you have to talk quite so loudly?"

"Sorry." Queen Dragon dropped her voice to a whisper. She took a closer look and realized that the girl wasn't an ordinary human after all. Even in the bad light she could see that her hair was silver and her skin an unusual shimmering gold. An extra hand rested on the edge of the cauldron and a fourth held the trident. Queen Dragon didn't care how many arms she had, but she did care, very much, about the magic cauldron. In Queen Dragon's experience, human attempts at magic usually meant trouble. Right now, more of that was the last thing she needed.

The girl took her hands away from her ears. "I'm Ariane," she announced. "The sea dragons told me you were stuck here. They got a bit out of control and whipped up this storm behind my back. Apparently you were shouting for help, but, when they called back, you couldn't hear them. I've come to rescue you. Hold your breath and jump into the sea."

"Jump into the sea?" Queen Dragon recoiled.

"The waves will smash me to bits in an instant! Help! Help! Anybody! *Help me!*"

A shimmering, whiskery face suddenly thrust out of the ocean, and Queen Dragon's cries turned into squawks of alarm. With a warlike shout, Ariane clanged her trident against the cauldron edge. Something huge nipped at Queen Dragon's toes and then at her tail. Queen Dragon shrieked, teetered, and flopped off the rock into the boiling sea.

On Skellig Lir the wind was still howling and the rain sheeted down. Lily lay pinioned under the tree, unable to move and barely able to feel anything. She felt sure all her bones ought to be broken and could hardly believe she was still alive.

The tree's branches covered her face, and she could smell the scent of its blossoms, pure and sweet like the flowers in the courtyard. It made her feel oddly safe. The storm's roar seemed strangely distant. Lily closed her eyes. Inside her head, she saw pictures of women weaving cloth on a loom, and of a marble-edged pool filled with pink and mauve flowers like the ones in the Drihtan's courtyard. Girls her own age were wading waist deep in the water, dipping huge skeins of white silk beneath the floating flowers. As the skeins came up, the color faded from the flowers and the skeins turned purple. A group of boys stood on the side of the pool with baskets, waiting to take the newly dyed silk away.

Moon roses, thought Lily. That's what the flowers are. Moon roses. A scatter of blossoms from the tree floated down onto her face, bringing with it such a waft of perfume that Lily felt as if she had died and gone to heaven. Then she heard human voices. The tree rustled its branches and parted them, and Lily felt a cold spatter of raindrops on her cheek.

"Lily?" A familiar golden face showed palely through the branches. Romina reached out a hand to brush aside Lily's hair, then turned and said something to her companions. The crown of the moon rose tree gave a great lurch upward. The next thing Lily knew, she was lying soaked in mud on the cold wet ground.

Lily yelled. It felt like sleeping in on a cold winter's morning and having all the blankets ripped off the bed. The tree swung momentarily over her head, and she saw that it was being pulled back by silken ropes wrapped around its trunk. A dozen golden-skinned women and girls were hauling expertly with their forty-eight hands. They swung the moon rose tree into an upright position, then ran up to it and eased it back into the earth where it had been ripped up.

The tree seemed to shake itself. Its roots sank back into the earth and the torn grass rolled back over them as if it had never been uprooted at all. The rescuers clapped their hands and cheered. Romina reached down and pulled Lily to her feet. Apart from a soaking, the experience had done her no harm. She was not so much as scratched or bruised.

"Come along, Lily," said Romina. "We had better get out of this rain."

The little party of rescuers was already heading off down a path toward a low white building. It had windows all down the side, and, as Lily and Romina followed the others, someone opened the door and beckoned them in. They hurried inside, scattering raindrops. Lily's rescuers crowded around her, pointing and staring at her pale skin and two arms.

A small stove burned in a corner with a cheerful glow, and the walls were hung with tapestries. Steaming teacups and little biscuits dusted with powdered sugar stood on a table off to one side, and a brass kettle boiled away merrily on the range top. An enormous loom, set with a web of purple cloth, almost filled the rest of the room. It was as if the weavers had been taking a tea break and were waiting for the light to come back when the great moon rose tree had fallen outside.

One of the girls closest to Lily suddenly gave a little cry.

"Aunt Berillian. Look!" She picked up one of the folds of Lily's mud-sodden fireproof cape and opened it out. At the sight of the gleaming fabric, a commotion broke out in the room. Romina stepped forward protectively. The tallest woman raised her hand to still the others.

"Yes, Jasmina. I see it," she said calmly. "I noticed as soon as we lifted the tree. Perhaps our visitor does not know what she is wearing."

Lily blushed with embarrassment. "I'm sorry,"

she said humbly. "I know it's very shabby, but it was already old when I got it. I have been through quite a lot with it since then."

A little woman with white hair and a lined face came over and laid a hand on Lily's arm. "Never mind, dear. I am sure that we can fix it. My name is Thalia. May I have a look?"

Lily took the cape off and passed it over. Thalia ran her twenty fingers over the material, seeking out the holes and scorched patches. She held the cape to her cheek and closed her eyes. After a few moments she smiled and laid it aside.

"The cape tells me it has not been back here for a hundred years or more," she said. "The last Quench who brought it for repairs was called Amy. The cape says she was your great-great-grandmother, Lily."

Lily was astonished. "The cape spoke to you?"

"The songs in the weave speak to the people who made them," explained Berillian. "Thalia would have worked on this cape when it was made. She is almost four hundred years old." She clapped her hands loudly above her head. "Back to work now, everyone. The storm is passing over, and our visitors will soon be on their way.

Jasmina, fetch Lily some clean clothes from the storeroom. The ones she is wearing are covered in mud."

The weavers turned back to the loom. Very soon the shuttles began flying again, and a song started up, following the same rhythm as the weaving. The music hung over the cloth like a pall of incense. Lily recognized the tune she had heard from a distance in the Drihtan's courtyard.

"What are they singing?" she asked Romina curiously. Jasmina returned with towels and a clean pink wool tunic with four sleeves to replace Lily's sodden dress. Romina helped Lily unbuckle her leather flying jacket and pull off her boots.

"They're weaving from silk dyed with the moon roses that grow on this island," Romina explained. "The moon roses are magic, and the dye makes the cloth magic, too. It can take the wearer under the water, through fire or the air, or even beyond it. It is said that, in the past, our people traveled to the moon and back again. It all depends on what the weavers sing into the cloth as it is woven."

"What are they singing now?"

"They are making flying capes," said Romina.

"Our people use them to travel between the islands, and the weavers are famous for them. And now, Lily, it is time for us to leave for the Outer Islands. The keeper of the Lighthouse of Skellig Mor is missing, and I need to search for her."

"I'm going, too?" Lily's heart leapt up at the thought of finding Queen Dragon. "Will we travel by bubble again?"

"Of course not." Romina pointed to the purple cloth on the loom. "We are going to fly!"

chapter five
The Cavern of Skellig Mor

Queen Dragon was swimming under the sea. It was horribly cold and dark. The water, churned up by the storm, swirled roughly around her, making the going very difficult. She had no idea where she was heading; she was simply following the leader and hoping she would end up safely somewhere as a result.

Ahead she could just make out the shadowy forms of four sea dragons and Ariane traveling in her cauldron like a little submarine. Normally

Queen Dragon was a strong swimmer, but this afternoon her weariness worked against her. Several times the sea dragons had to pause so she could catch up. Their whiskery faces were so gentle it was hard to imagine they were the same creatures who had nearly drowned dozens of sailors earlier in the day. Queen Dragon could tell that they were talking to one another, but their language and method of communication was silent, and she had no idea what they were saying. It occurred to her, rather sadly, that the sea dragons, who were so closely related to her own kind, were in fact more alien to her than most of her friends in Ashby.

You've spent too much time with humans, Sinhault, Queen Dragon told herself. *You need the company of dragons.* An unwanted picture popped briefly into her head, of herself and Serpentine Bridgestock sitting on a crag in the long-lost country of the dragons; of a huge golden dragon flying toward them and her excitement sending fireballs shooting from her nostrils. There was no excitement now, only sadness, for Serpentine was dead, and the golden dragon, who had once meant more to her than all the rest put together, had been lost for thousands of years. Four thousand years was a very long time to be collecting memories. Queen Dragon was now almost the last of her kind, and it was a melancholy position to be in.

At last they started swimming upward. The darkness became briefly much darker, and then Queen Dragon saw a dim light shimmering up ahead, as if the surface of the water was pierced by sunlight. With the last of her strength, she struck out toward the light, and her head and neck broke through into fresh air.

A cave. Queen Dragon felt an immediate rush of relief. She liked caves, and, frankly, anywhere was better than under the ocean. This was a sea cavern, for she could hear waves booming against the rocks and the rattling roar of water hitting a shingly beach somewhere close by. There was a huge cleft in the rock overhead that let in both daylight and rain. It was still pouring, but the lightning and thunder seemed to have lessened, and the storm was finally passing overhead. Queen Dragon wallowed in the shallows, her own weight suddenly seeming too much for her to carry. With one last supreme effort, she staggered out onto a patch of rock and pebble and collapsed.

Behind her the four sea dragons swam around the cavern, ducking and diving and blowing water through their nostrils. Ariane beached the cauldron and secured it to a rock with a rope. She took off her helmet and shook out her hair, then ran on dainty bare feet across the rocks, dodging the rain until she could shelter under an overhanging outcropping near Queen Dragon's head.

"Sorry to be a pest," Queen Dragon said plaintively, "but I'm awfully hungry. Do you think I could have something to eat?"

"I hadn't thought about that." Ariane looked around the cavern. "There's nothing down here. But we can go up to the beach in a little while, when the rain slackens. There's some fish in the tank for the sea dragons' dinner. Captain Rhemus delivered it this morning, so it's quite fresh."

"Fish!" said Queen Dragon in a weak but scornful voice. "What do you want to do—poison me? In case it has escaped your notice, I am not a sea dragon, I am a winged land serpent. *Draco magnus,* if you want to get technical, Queen

Dragon to my friends. *My* kind of dragon eats metal."

"Metal?"

"Yes." Queen Dragon felt her tummy rumble. "I don't suppose you've got any handy?"

"Only my boat," said Ariane, "and you're not having that. I'll send the sea dragons to see if they can find something for you. There's all sorts of stuff lying about on the ocean floor." She turned to the sea dragons, who were still frolicking about the cavern. At once they stopped and, after a moment, sank down again into the water. Interested, Queen Dragon watched their wake heading out of the cavern.

"I suppose they're telepathic," she remarked. "No point in talking when you spend most of your life underwater. Can you speak their language?"

"Yes. That's why they sent me here to Skellig Mor," said Ariane. "When the old lighthouse keeper died, the people on Skellig Lir searched all the islands in the archipelago for his replacement. I was the one who scored highest in the tests, so they stuck me out here on this rock in the middle of nowhere and told me I could never go home."

"Dear me," said Queen Dragon. "That does sound a bit grim. What do you have to do?"

"Nothing," said Ariane bitterly. "I light the lamp, feed the sea dragons, and keep them from whipping up storms and attacking ships. Every day a fishing boat comes with a new load of fish. The rest of the time, I just sit around on the rocks and look at the sea, and I hate it, I hate it, *I hate it!*" Her voice rose vehemently, echoing off the cavern walls, and she smashed her four small fists against the rock.

Queen Dragon opened her mouth, then closed it again. Her dragon's intuition told her that something here was very wrong. Ariane, and this situation, was going to need careful handling.

"It certainly does sound a little dull," she agreed at last. "I'm surprised they haven't found someone else to help you with the job. Have you tried talking to the sea dragons about it? They do seem as if they're rather attached to you."

Ariane's face softened momentarily. "Yes. I think they understand how I feel. But they're not like you, Queen Dragon. They can't talk or hold a conversation; they just send you pictures of what they're thinking or how they're feeling. And when there's a lot of them and they're agitated, the way they are now . . ." Ariane fell silent. "Queen Dragon, I'm frightened. In the last few weeks, new sea dragons have been coming to Skellig Mor from every direction. I've never seen so many of them. And I've been having dreams, horrible dreams. I keep seeing this huge whirlpool out in the straits. It's black and deep, as if it's made of glass, and it spins down into nothing so you can't see the bottom. In my dream I'm getting sucked into it, and all I can do is scream and scream and scream." She clasped her four hands together and Queen Dragon saw that they were shaking. "Queen Dragon, I've got to get away from here. I can't sleep, I can't even think. Half the time the sea dragons won't do what I tell them. Please help me. If I stay on Skellig Mor, I know I shall go mad!"

Queen Dragon digested this long speech in silence. She was not sure what to make of it. She was not even sure whether Ariane was telling the truth or, at any rate, the whole truth. She did not strike her as a very trustworthy sort of girl, and the unsolved mystery of where the magic boat had come from was still very much in the back of Queen Dragon's mind. But she could not speak of these concerns to Ariane. There was no doubting she was genuinely very upset.

"But what about the sea dragons?" Queen Dragon said at last. "Isn't it your job, your duty, to look after them? Who will feed them and keep them from attacking ships and making storms? Won't they be disappointed if you just disappear?"

"The Drihtan will find someone else," said Ariane. "He'll have to. And the sea dragons can manage by themselves. They'll miss me a bit at first, and I'll miss them, too. But I simply can't stay here on Skellig Mor a moment longer."

"Of course, I'm always happy to help anyone in trouble," said Queen Dragon, after a pause. "But I'm not quite sure what you want me to do."

"I should have thought it was obvious," said Ariane. "Fly me off the island, of course."

"Fly you off the island?" Queen Dragon was taken aback. "But where to? If I take you to

Skellig Lir, won't they just make you come straight back here?"

"Oh, I don't want you to take me *there*," said Ariane. "No. It's got to be farther away than that. I'll leave it to you to decide, Queen Dragon. You must have traveled a lot. You'll know all the good places."

"You mean you want to leave the archipelago?" The full thrust of what Ariane was saying was finally sinking into Queen Dragon's skull. Her dorsal scales stood up on end, a sure sign she was feeling agitated. Queen Dragon had thought that Ariane was just thoughtless and irresponsible. It had not occurred to her that she was entirely lacking in common sense as well.

"Of course I want to leave. There's nothing for me here. I'm an orphan, you know. My parents had a fishing boat. They were washed overboard and drowned in a big storm when I was only a baby."

"I'm sorry to hear that." It occurred to Queen Dragon that Ariane did not sound especially sorry herself, but she was so self-absorbed that perhaps that was not surprising. By now Queen Dragon's head was spinning, and she scarcely knew what to say. "Ariane, has it ever occurred to you that life outside the archipelago might be . . . different?"

"I suppose it has to be," said Ariane carelessly. "Well, it stands to reason, doesn't it? I don't mind, though. Anything's got to be better than staying here."

"As a matter of fact, you're wrong," said Queen Dragon. "My dear, I have every sympathy for you, but I assure you, there are many worse places to be than Skellig Mor. The people in the outside world are not like those in the archipelago. Most of them would stare at you, some would be unkind, and a few would be worse than unkind if they got the chance. I am sorry to say," said Queen Dragon, warming to her theme, "that there are human beings who would actually lock you up in a cage and put you on display in a sideshow. You would probably make them very rich. They would certainly make you very miserable."

"Oh." Ariane had gone quiet. "What's a sideshow?"

"It's a place where human beings go to see unusual things, or other people who look a bit different," said Queen Dragon. "I'm sorry, Ariane.

Most human beings would take one look at your four arms and golden skin and run screaming in the opposite direction."

"But why?" asked Ariane. "I'm not a freak. How many arms do Outsiders have, anyway?"

"Only two," said Queen Dragon, "and they are generally shades of brown or pink. Rather drab, by dragon standards. But I think you can see why it is not a good idea for you to get mixed up with them. I would hate to fly you out of here if it got you into trouble."

Ariane started to cry. "But I want to leave! I must! Please, Queen Dragon. You're my only chance!"

Queen Dragon shifted uncomfortably. She hated it when people cried, for despite her fierce appearance she was very soft-hearted. She tried to speak as firmly as she could. "No, Ariane, I can't," she said. "I'm very sorry, but it would be irresponsible and wrong of me. Speak to the people who put you here and see if they can find you a companion. Besides," she finished up, "I can't leave the archipelago anyway. I came here with a friend, and she's gone missing. Until she's found, I am not going anywhere."

"Who's your friend?" asked Ariane. "I might be able to tell you where to find her."

"Her name is Lily," said Queen Dragon. "Lily Quench."

"Lily Quench." Ariane repeated the name as if she was committing it to memory. Suddenly she looked up. Above the thrumming of the rain a bell could be heard ringing somewhere overhead. Queen Dragon, whose eyes saw equally well by day or night, now realized that the gloom in the cavern was no longer due to the storm. Night was falling, and it was getting dark.

"The lighthouse bell," said Ariane. "It's reminding me that it's time to light the lamp."

chapter six
Lily on the Wing

The storm was passing overhead as a newly dry Lily followed Romina and Berillian out of the weavers' workroom into the garden. In her arms Berillian carried two long folded pieces of cloth. The material was purple and crimson, like an old-fashioned rose, a similar color to Lily's fireproof cape, though much more lightweight and finely woven.

Romina looked up at the sky. "The rain has not quite stopped," she said, "but it will be gone very soon. Lily, since you are so concerned about your friend, Queen Dragon, I think it would be best for you to come with me and search for her yourself. Berillian has a new flying cape for you. Most of our people are expert fliers. In the old days, people from the outside world used to think that we had wings."

"It's beautiful." Lily reached out and stroked the cape Berillian was holding. The fabric crackled under her hands, and she felt a little fizz of electricity go shooting through her body and out her fingertips. The sensation was invigorating, like jumping into a cold pool for a swim on a very hot day, and immediately Lily felt excited at the prospect of putting it on.

Berillian draped the hooded flying cape around Lily's shoulders and fastened it with a silver pin.

"This brooch holds the cape in place while you're flying," she explained. "Whatever you do, don't undo it until you're on the ground again. Your hands go here, like this." She helped Lily put her hands through two slits near the hem and fastened buckles around her wrists to secure them in place. A strange light feeling started rippling through Lily's body. She found herself rising up unexpectedly on tiptoes and swaying back and forth like an anchored balloon.

"Take care," laughed Berillian. "You don't want to take off too close to the building."

Romina buckled on her own cape and stepped off the path onto a square patch of grass between two flower beds. She bent her knees like a diver and pointed her hands above her head. Then she pushed off with her feet and rose gracefully through the cool air, bringing her hands slowly down by her side and coming to a halt just above Berillian's head.

"Wow!" Lily tried to copy Romina's movements, but a neat take-off was not as easy as it looked. She shot up off the ground at an odd angle, tried to right herself, and tipped upside down, her long pink tunic flopping down around her ears.

"Oops!" Lily flapped at her skirts with her hands, but she had forgotten she was still wearing the flying cape and her movements only succeeded in making her lurch into the nearby wall. She flailed around a moment longer, unable to see. Romina flew over, pulled her out from under the building's eaves, and deftly flipped her upright.

"Try to think of yourself as swimming through the air," she advised. "It's not that hard. Remember, the flying cape does most of the work for you. Just fix your eyes on where you want to go and strike out toward it, like this." She reached out with her four hands and glided gracefully away across the meadow.

Lily hung in the air, watching her go. It looked like tremendous fun, but she could not quite believe she would be able to do it herself. Then she looked down and realized that, quite unconsciously, she was treading water in midair. She stopped, and immediately started sinking back down to the ground. Lily kicked back up again. She pushed out with her arms as if doing the breaststroke and made a scissoring motion with her legs. This time the cape billowed out around her and, to her astonishment, she found herself gliding after Romina across the wet grass.

"See!" shouted Romina. "It's not so hard, is it?"

"I think I'm getting the hang of it." Lily struck out again and shot forward, gathering height and speed with every stroke. Before she knew it she was above the trees, and the whole island of Skellig Lir was opening out beneath her. She could see orchards of moon roses, neat round houses, and flowery terraces; even the Drihtan's palace, curled up like a golden shell in a fold of the land. They crossed the coastline and passed over the tiny island where the library was. Then Skellig Lir was behind them, and they were skimming out with the clouds over the open sea.

"I can't believe the storm has cleared so quickly," said Lily as they flew along. The air was cool and a bit bumpy, but she had encountered far worse turbulence flying with Queen Dragon and was not finding the going unduly difficult. The dark clouds were already breaking up, and she could see small patches of blue sky to the north.

"They used to call the archipelago the Fairweather Isles," said Romina. "You still see the name on old maps. But it is true that bad weather passes over quickly here. When we come back to Skellig Lir, you'll find there's no trace of storm damage at all. It's part of the magic of these islands."

"I see," said Lily, though she wasn't entirely sure

she did. The whole issue of magic seemed to be very important here. The islands in the archipelago were magic, and the Library of Skellig Lir was full of magical books. Yet, despite the flying capes, the magical moon rose trees, the wonders of the Drihtan's palace, there seemed to be no actual magicians. Who used the magical library then? Altogether it was a puzzle, and one Lily knew she had to work out before she could answer the librarian's question and find out what she needed to know about closing off the Eye Stones.

For the moment it would have to wait: it was more important to find Queen Dragon. Lily tried to concentrate on staying airborne and keeping on course. Now I really know what it must be like to be a dragon, Lily thought. If only Queen Dragon could see me now! She closed her eyes briefly and pictured herself soaring off alongside Queen Dragon. The sensation was a bit like swimming and a bit like falling, and, as the wind whipped past Lily's body and pushed up under her flying cape, she found herself swaying and dipping with the air currents like a bird. It was hard to resist the temptation to go flying off by herself and turn somersaults in midair. The whole experience was so exciting, all she wanted to do was shriek with joy.

"You're doing well, Lily," said Romina. "Most new fliers take much longer to get the hang of it."

"I've done a lot of flying with Queen Dragon," said Lily. "I guess I must have picked things up from her without realizing." Mentioning Queen Dragon's name aloud reminded her why she was flying to the Outer Islands, and some of the thrill of the experience evaporated.

"We're making reasonably good progress," Romina said. "The wind is blowing in the wrong direction because of the storm, but we should still be at Skellig Mor by nightfall."

"Is that where Queen Dragon disappeared?" asked Lily.

Romina shook her head. "No. But it's nearby. Skellig Mor is the home of Ariane, the lighthouse keeper who has gone missing. It's her job to look after the sea dragons and keep them under control. Otherwise they run wild and attack ships, or whip up storms. They are magical creatures and need careful handling. The keeper of the

Lighthouse of Skellig Mor has one of the most important jobs in the whole archipelago. Ariane should be proud she has been chosen. Instead, she has done nothing but let us down ever since she was appointed."

"Can you find someone else?" asked Lily.

"Ariane can communicate with the sea dragons," explained Romina. "It is a very rare gift. We've promised we'll send an assistant as soon as we find someone suitable, but she seems to think everyone on Skellig Lir has forgotten her. This is the fourth time she has tried to run away. Twice she tried to fly off the island, and we had to confiscate her flying cape. Then she disguised herself as a fishergirl and hid on the boat that brings the fish in for the sea dragons. This time she's just vanished. I'm not sure where she's gone."

"What about the boats from the outside world?" asked Lily. "Could she have stowed away on one of those?"

"You mean the moon rose thieves?" Romina sounded shocked. "Oh, no. Surely Ariane wouldn't . . . she couldn't be so stupid." She sounded very agitated. "The sea dragons are our chief protection against invasion from the outside world. If Ariane makes contact with Outsiders, it means they have the means to control the sea dragons. It means they could come pouring into the archipelago, and we would be powerless to stop them!"

Queen Dragon sat in the cove on the eastern side of Skellig Mor, waiting for Ariane to light the lamp. They had left the undersea cavern almost half an hour ago and, though this far south it took a long time to get completely dark, what remained of the twilight was rapidly fading. There were still storm clouds in the sky and the odd flash of lightning, but they were far away to the south.

Behind her, a squat square tower stood among the rocks of the foreshore: the lighthouse where Ariane lived. Queen Dragon did not understand why it was taking her so long to light the lamp, and an uneasy thought crossed her mind— perhaps Ariane had taken the opportunity to abscond. But at length a pearly glow appeared at the very top of the tower and swept over the beach, just bright enough for human eyes to see by. A few minutes later Ariane came out of the lighthouse door and scrambled down over the rocks.

"There," she said. "At least they can't complain I'm not doing my job. The light gets brighter as the night goes on. The sea dragons will come in around midnight and go back out to sea at dawn."

"I see." Queen Dragon tried to turn the conversation to something that had been preying on her thoughts. "Ariane, about your cauldron. It's most unusual. I was wondering where it came from."

"Oh, I found it in the cavern," said Ariane. "One day, not long after I arrived here, there was a tremendous roar, like an explosion. Some of the rocks above the cavern had collapsed down into it, making the hole in the roof. I went down on a rope and explored: it's my secret place. Unless you're standing right above the cavern and looking down through the hole in the rock, you wouldn't even know it was there."

"But the cauldron is surely very special,"

persisted Queen Dragon. "How do you suppose it got into the cavern?"

"I don't know," said Ariane. "It's magic, of course. I think it must have been in the cavern for a very long time. I've tried to sail away in it, but the sea dragons won't let me. By the way, Queen Dragon, you must promise never to tell anyone the cavern's there. Nobody knows about it except you."

"I promise," said Queen Dragon. She looked up and saw a purple glimmer in the sky. Though she did not know why, her spirits suddenly surged. The purple object reappeared, this time catching the light from the lighthouse lamp. A second appeared behind it and, like two streaks of purple flame, they headed down toward the beach.

"Flying capes!" gasped Ariane. "Oh no! They've come to get me!" And she turned and ran for the rocks.

Lily flew down toward the Lighthouse of Skellig Mor, the light from the lamp catching unexpected

highlights in her magical cape. Ahead she could
see Romina's cape, spread out in flight like a
floating net of purple glowworms. Lily followed
her as closely as she could, making for the beach
in the cove. The tower and the island looked
oddly familiar, and she realized she and Queen
Dragon must have flown over it on their
approach that morning. She must have been too
busy worrying about the sea dragons to have
really noticed it.

The beach was getting closer, and Lily could
hear waves breaking on the shore. Suddenly she
realized they were about to land, and she didn't
know how to.

"Romina! Help! What do I do?"

She shouted and flapped her arms, but Romina
could not hear for the wind and the waves. Lily
tried to remember how Queen Dragon landed,
but it was hard to think straight in an emergency.
She saw Romina's arms float up and fold in
neatly at her sides, and tried to follow her.

"Help! *Help!*"

Sparking and glittering like a purple firecracker,
Lily pulled in her arms and started to fall. Too
late, she flapped, but the ground came up

unexpectedly, and there was no time to stop. There was a crunch, a jarring bounce that juddered through her body. The flying cape billowed up around her in a tangle, and she pitched with a helpless cry toward the shingle.

chapter seven
Skellig Mor

"Ow!" Lily flung out her hands to save herself. But before she could fall on the treacherous pebbles a huge wave hit her from behind. It washed her up the beach, then dumped her. Lily rolled over in the surf, spluttering and swallowing cold salt water. The wave started going out, rushing back against her long skirts and almost ripping the flying cape from her shoulders.

Another wave roared, coming in behind her. Lily got up and started hurrying as best she could out of its reach. Her long tunic and boots had protected her from serious injury, but they were so heavy with water she could hardly walk. The second wave caught her in the shallows, rushing around her knees and washing the pebbles from under her feet as it receded. When it had gone, Lily picked up her skirts and soggy flying cape and squelched forward out of the water and up the beach.

"Lily!" A large red shape emerged from behind a cluster of rocks and waddled toward her. "Are you all right?"

Lily gave a cry of joy. "Queen Dragon! You're alive!"

"Yes. Which is more than you deserve to be," said Queen Dragon reprovingly. "My dear, I've never seen a worse landing in my entire life! Whatever will you be up to next?"

"I only learned to fly this afternoon," said Lily. "Don't be cross, Queen Dragon. I've done really well up until now." The lamplight swept across the beach, and she saw Romina standing nearby. "Queen Dragon, this is Romina. She's here to look for the lighthouse keeper who's gone missing. And I came to look for you. I've been so worried. I thought you'd drowned in that storm."

"I nearly did drown," said Queen Dragon. "But I found my way safely to this island, and here I am. As for the lighthouse keeper, she's up in the rocks somewhere. She ran away when she saw you coming in to land."

"I'm sure she did. She has made a habit of it." Romina sighed. "Though I see the lamp has been lit, so maybe things aren't as bad as they seem." She took off her flying cape and deftly folded it away into a purse at her waist. Then she produced two pairs of glasses in green frames.

"I'm afraid I have no dry clothes, Lily," she said. "But if you put these on, you'll find they help you see as well at night as in the day, and over longer than normal distances, too. Ariane will have clean clothes in the lighthouse. If you can help me find her, you should be able to borrow some of her things."

Lily hung her flying cape over a nearby rock to dry. She and Romina walked together up the beach. The island was a honeycomb of rocks and crannies, and, even wearing night glasses, Lily could tell it would be hard to find someone who knew the island as well as Ariane must. After a while, Romina put her flying cape back on again and flew over the island in a series of sweeping passes. But she had no success. She had just come back to report when the circling beam of light from the lighthouse tower suddenly faltered and went out.

"Look!" Lily pointed. "What happened?"

Romina took to the air again and circled the tower, peering in through the window. A few moments later she landed beside Lily, her cape, four arms, and glasses making her look unnervingly like a large purple butterfly.

"I can't see anything," she said. "But we'll have to do something about it. The tide is coming in, and soon the sea dragons will arrive. Without the light to guide them, they'll run themselves up onto the rocks beneath the headland and get hurt." She took off her cape and folded it up. Lily noticed a small stream trickling down a rock. She went over and cupped her hands for a drink.

"Would you like something to eat?" Romina fished in her purse and produced a small piece of fruit that looked a bit like a pear with silvery green skin. Lily polished it on her sleeve and eagerly bit into it, for she was indeed very hungry. As her teeth sank into the flesh a horrible bitter-tasting juice flooded her mouth and she nearly spat it out. But then the taste grew smoother and sweeter, until at last it was like honey sliding over her tongue. When she took the next bite, it was delicious.

"It tastes bad at first because you are used to food from the outside world," said Romina, biting into a pear of her own. "It has spoiled your sense of taste. If you lived here in the archipelago, you would be shocked at the food you are used to eating."

Lily nibbled down to the pear's core. "Everything seems special here. The plants, the weather, the people. It's as if everything is extra . . . alive somehow."

"That's because it is more alive," said Romina. "The archipelago is one of the few places left that are close to the way they were when the world was new. There are not many now. Most of them have filled up with people and become spoiled."

"The Singing Wood is like that," said Lily. "I went there last year with Queen Dragon and met my grandmother. I wanted to stay with her in the forest and never leave, but it wasn't allowed."

"I have heard of the Singing Wood," said Romina, "though I have never been there. I believe there is also a hidden valley in the mountains of the uttermost northwest, but human beings rarely go there, and I do not know much about it. Have you finished eating, Lily? We must go and fix the lamp."

Lily wiped her sticky fingers on her tunic. It was starting to dry out a bit, but the salt was making the material stiff and itchy, and she longed for a clean set of clothes. She followed Romina up the rocks and along a path to the back door of the lighthouse. They let themselves in, and Romina took off her glasses and turned up an oil lamp that had been left burning on the kitchen table.

"What a mess!" she said, clicking her tongue. The lighthouse kitchen smelled strongly of fish and grease and rubbish. It was frowzy and unloved; there was garbage on the floor, and the fire in the grate had burned out, leaving nothing but ashes. Yet, with its cream walls and pretty blue and yellow curtains, it should have been extremely homey. Lily knew that if it had been hers, it would have looked cheerful and welcoming. Ariane obviously didn't care or even want to try.

The rest of the lighthouse was no better. Upstairs was a parlor full of dirt and cobwebs, and above it a depressing bedroom. There was a bed under the window that hadn't been made, and an old rag rug on the floor. Someone had been playing ticktacktoe on the wall in chalk and not even bothered to rub it out.

"Honestly. That girl never does a thing to make this place comfortable," said Romina disapprovingly. "Look at that: bed unmade, dirty clothes tossed on the floor. And then she complains that she hates being here! If she would only try to make things nice, it wouldn't be so bad." She took some trousers and a shirt out of a wardrobe and handed them to Lily. "Here, Lily. I don't think Ariane will mind your borrowing these. You get changed; I'm going upstairs to look at the lamp."

Lily nodded. Romina's footsteps sounded on the spiral stairs that led up to the lamp room. A moment later Lily heard things grating and shifting around overhead. She put on the clothes, which were not as clean as she would have liked, and tied the extra set of sleeves around her waist. Lily was just popping her night glasses into the pocket of Ariane's trousers when she glimpsed something moving out of the window.

"Lily? Are you there?" Romina's voice sounded down the staircase. Lily ran up the steps and poked her head into the lamp room. Romina was sitting on the floor with a large drip tray full of filthy-looking oil.

"This is going to take me a little while," she said. "Ariane can't have cleaned the lamp in months. I'm going to have to drain it and put new oil into the reservoir. Would you like to stay and help? Or would you rather go back to Queen Dragon?"

"I might keep looking for Ariane," said Lily. "I thought I saw something move down in the rocks. But I didn't have my night glasses on, and I couldn't be sure."

"Take care then," said Romina. "If you're not back here first, I'll meet you on the beach with Queen Dragon in about a quarter of an hour."

Lily went back down the stairs and left the

lighthouse. Her heart was beating as she put on
her night glasses and walked up the path into the
rocks. She could not be sure that she really had
seen Ariane moving behind the lighthouse, but,
just in case, she tried to walk as quietly as her
booted feet would let her. Then she heard it: a
soft whistle along the path ahead of her. Lily froze
on the spot, her brain whirling with choices as
she tried to decide what to do.

Was Ariane calling her? Lily had no idea
whether there was anyone else on the island, but
obviously someone had seen her. If she went back
to the lighthouse, whoever it was might run away
again. Lily walked cautiously forward, looking
behind rocks as she went, and then she heard
another call a little way along the path. The
mysterious whistler was moving away from her,
calling her to follow.

"Ariane? Ariane, is that you?" Lily called out
as loudly as she dared. But this time there was
no answering whistle, and, in a few more paces,
the path gave out. Lily stepped up onto an
outcropping and tried to peer into a hollow
between two rocks.

"Ariane!"

Suddenly a bright light swept across the rocks, dazzling her night glasses. Lily spun around and felt her foot skid in a patch of gravel. She heard something move behind her, and somebody gave her a vicious shove in the back. Then the light swept out to sea again, and she fell forward into the darkness.

chapter eight
Skeletons from the Past

Everything happened so quickly Lily had scarcely realized she'd been ambushed before she hit cold water. Rats! she thought as she plunged down and tasted salt. That's the third time today I've been soaked! I've only just got changed! Her night glasses were dangling from one ear, and she had just enough presence of mind to grab them before they fell off and were lost for good. Holding them tightly in her hand, Lily kicked and swam back up to the surface.

"Hey! Is anyone up there?" Lily shook her wet

hair out of her eyes and trod water. When she put the night glasses back on her nose, she saw that she was inside a cave. Most of it was full of water, but there was a section of gravel off to one side. Lily struck out toward it and was soon able to touch the bottom. There was a cleft in the rocks overhead through which she had obviously fallen, but it was a long way up, and she could see nothing through it but a few stars and the regular sweep of the lighthouse lamp.

"Romina! Queen Dragon! Can you hear me?" Lily's voice echoed off the rocks, but there was no reply. She looked around the cavern. A round boat, or what looked like one, had been dragged up onto the shingle and fastened by a rope to a nearby boulder. Lily's spirits lifted when she saw it, but only for a moment. The cavern walls went down to the water on all other sides. There did not seem to be any way of getting the boat out.

"How strange." The boat had obviously been brought into the cavern somehow, but Lily could not immediately think of an explanation. She thought mournfully of her flying cape, spread out to dry down on the beach. If she had been wearing it, she could have flown out without any difficulty at all. Still, the island was not very big, and it seemed likely that if she kept shouting someone would hear. Somebody had to. Trapped in the cavern without food or fresh water, if no one came to find her, she would soon meet with a very miserable end.

Down on the beach, Queen Dragon was enjoying a well-deserved snooze. Her internal fires had rekindled, and smoke seeped from her nostrils while she slept. A comforting fog now covered the beach around her for a considerable distance. She snored, dreaming of shining mounds of metal garnished with golden coins, a dragon banquet laid out in a gigantic cavern under the earth. Queen Dragon was just deciding what to eat first when her rest was interrupted by booted footsteps crunching toward her. A voice called her name. Queen Dragon sighed and wrinkled her nose in sleep. Her mouth worked, and, after a moment, she opened her left eye a crack and peered through it.

"Queen Dragon. Is Lily around?" An indistinct

figure stood in front of her, swathed in smoke. Queen Dragon took several seconds to identify the voice as Romina's.

"No. She's not. I thought she was with you."

"I've been fixing the lamp. I told Lily I'd meet her down on the beach. She must still be looking for Ariane." Romina took out her flying cape and put it on. "Queen Dragon, I'm going to leave now and do an aerial search of the neighboring islands. If Lily arrives, will you tell her where I am?"

"Of course." Queen Dragon watched Romina fly away. She let her eyes droop shut again, but it was hard to go back to sleep. The lighthouse lamp kept flashing across her face, and part of her was now listening out for Lily. A little tickle of anxiety started protruding into Queen Dragon's thoughts. Since Lily's arrival at the lighthouse she had hardly seen her, and Queen Dragon did not think it was Lily's job to go looking for Ariane, whom she did not trust anyway. Smoke poured from her nostrils as it always did when she was worried. Then she heard a second, lighter set of footsteps on the pebbly beach, and saw a small figure in a hooded flying cape walking toward her through the fog.

"Lily!" Queen Dragon shook herself properly awake. "Where have you been? Did you find Ariane? Romina's just flown off to look for her on some nearby islands."

"Oh. Has she?" A particularly thick cloud of smoke came puffing from Queen Dragon's nose, and Lily coughed loudly. She flapped the flying cape's edge across her face and spoke in a muffled voice. "Ariane was er . . . in the lighthouse. I've just said good-bye to her. She'll wait there until Romina comes back."

"I wouldn't count on that," said Queen Dragon darkly. "Still. She's not our problem. Did you find what you wanted on Skellig Lir?" There was another little gush of smoke, and, again, Lily started coughing. She nodded vigorously, however, and patted her hip as if something was hidden in a pocket under the cape. Delighted, Queen Dragon sat up and shook out her wings.

"Tremendous! Let's go home then and give those Eye Stones what for!"

"This is ridiculous," said Lily aloud. Trapped in the cavern, she was starting to get more and more anxious. No one seemed to be hearing her shouts for help. Worse, neither Queen Dragon nor Romina seemed to have even noticed she was missing.

There was one certain way of being rescued. Before their adventure in the Black Mountains, Queen Dragon had taught Lily the Dragons' Cry of Summoning. The cry was a magical call that would summon aid to any dragon in distress; if Queen Dragon was still within earshot, she would come as soon as it was made. But Queen Dragon had impressed upon Lily that the Dragons' Cry of Summoning could be used only in the case of direst need, and Lily was not convinced that her present situation was desperate enough. Used carelessly, the cry could be dangerous. If no other dragons were near enough to hear, it could recoil on the person in need of help and kill her.

For what seemed like the hundredth time, Lily shouted Queen Dragon's name.

"Queen Dragon! It's me, Lily, can you hear?"

A flapping sounded from the direction of the beach, the unmistakable beat of giant wings laboring in take-off. Queen Dragon had heard her! Elated, Lily jumped up and down and shouted again as loudly as she could.

"Down here, Queen Dragon! I'm in the cavern; look down here!" A huge flying shadow passed over the hole in the cavern roof. Lily saw a human figure in a purple flying cape perched on Queen Dragon's head and screamed again at the top of her lungs. But the sound of flapping wings grew fainter. It took several moments for Lily to realize they were not coming back. Queen Dragon was not circling the island but heading up beyond the clouds to ride the air currents. She had flown away.

Lily was stunned. At first she could hardly react at all. Then she sank down on the shingle and began to gulp back tears. Never before had Queen Dragon abandoned her. Never before had she failed to come to her aid. Lily could only assume some dreadful emergency must have arisen. Perhaps Romina had needed to return to Skellig Lir, and Queen Dragon had offered to fly her back there quickly, or maybe they were chasing after Ariane. Lily didn't care. All she knew was that Queen Dragon had left her. Chances were neither she nor Romina had even realized Lily was missing before they went.

"There must be a way out; there must!" Lily kicked the metal boat with her boot and banged it with her fists, then leaned against it and burst into storms of weeping. What was the use of having a boat in a cavern where you couldn't use it? She was going to die alone and forgotten in the darkness, with nothing but a useless metal tub for company. Furthermore, the water in the cave, being seawater, was behaving like seawater and getting deeper. The tide was coming in so fast that Lily would soon have nowhere to stand.

The boat had to have been brought into the cavern somehow. Lily forced herself to calm down and try to think. It was possible, of course, that the boat had come in when the tide was much lower than it was now. In that case, the exit would now be *under* the surface of the water. Lily straightened her night glasses on her nose and determinedly scanned the cavern walls. Sure enough, about halfway along the western side a darkish line showed against the water, like the very top of a tunnel opening.

Lily waded back into the water. Keeping her

night glasses firmly in place, she dog-paddled over to the opposite side of the cavern. As she swam closer she noticed the shadow growing more distinct. It was indeed a low opening and, to her delight, on the other side was a spacious, water-filled passage. Lily ducked under the curtain of rock and continued swimming along the passage. After a bit she rounded a bend and came to a rocky ledge sloping up out of the water into darkness.

Lily pulled herself out of the water and pressed on, following her instinct and heading for higher ground wherever she could. The way before her broke up quickly into a honeycomb of little passages, all looking and smelling more or less the same. The first went only a little way into the rock before petering out. The second was far too tight for even Lily's small body to cram into, but a third was more promising. After an initial squeeze it opened out into a tall passage about as wide as Lily's shoulders, and continued to lead upward, eventually coming out into a small cave filled with rocks, gravel, and debris.

The sea was booming somewhere ahead, so Lily guessed she must be headed in the right direction. But the way before her was steep, and by now she was feeling tired. Lily sat down on a clump of rocks to rest. Immediately something hard and sharp stuck into her leg and there was a snapping noise, like a piece of dry stick breaking in two. With a little scream, Lily threw herself forward, scattering gravel. Something round and bony came rattling down out of the outcropping, and she kicked out at it like a football, sending it spinning off into the darkness.

It was a human skull.

The echo of Lily's own screams bouncing off the walls almost deafened her. All her sensible Quench blood seemed to drain out of her body in an instant, and she ran skittering backward as if the skull was snapping at her heels. A skeleton was hidden in the rocks, and she had sat down on it in the darkness! Several moments passed before Lily could bring herself even to look. The bones were lying in a little cleft, and a knife stood out among the clutter of ribs and vertebrae. It was a horrible-looking thing, made out of greenish metal with a black hilt and writing on the blade. Lily went to pick it up, then stopped. Her left arm, with its magical covering of dragonlike scales, had begun to tingle furiously.

It was the same sort of warning she had felt when she had met the witch, Aunt Cassy, at the Castle of Mote Ely. Lily did not understand why, but it was much stronger than the tingling she normally felt when her life was threatened, like a sort of supernatural lightning shooting up her arm. And the knife was responsible. In such a damp place, Lily was sure an ordinary knife ought to have rusted, but this one gleamed dully, without a spot or mark. It must be magic, left behind by some unknown visitor to the island. As for the skeleton . . . there was only one set of arm bones, making it plain that whoever it was had come from outside the archipelago. A small detail came unexpectedly back to Lily: that the magicians who had despoiled the magical library had traveled to Skellig Lir in iron cauldrons. Lily thought of the boat she had seen in the cavern and wondered whether the magicians had been to Skellig Mor, too.

Someone had been killed here long ago. But over what? Lily's foot nudged something in the darkness, and she bent down and picked it up.

It was a book. The cover had once been bright, but it was now dark, with a faint iridescence like an insect skin that had been shed and abandoned in the garden. But there was still enough magic about it for her to recognize where it had come from. With trembling hands, Lily wiped the dirt off the cover and opened it.

The first forty pages were missing, except for half a page showing a picture of an eye carved on a black pointed rock in the middle of an empty landscape. A few stubby little edges of paper still stuck up mutely from the spine, but the rest of the section had been completely torn out. The thief had simply ripped out the chapters he or she was interested in and thrown away the rest of the book as trash. Worst of all, it looked as if they had destroyed the very book Lily had wanted to read herself.

A feeling of sick disappointment rose up in Lily's throat. The books she had been shown in the Drihtan's throne room had been among the most beautiful things she had ever seen in her life. She could not imagine how anyone could possibly want to destroy one. Even the remaining pages were so damaged they were virtually illegible. As Lily turned the page with the picture of the Eye Stone on it, it crumbled away into little flakes between her fingers.

Her quest to close off the Eye Stones looked to have finished right here. All she could do was take what was left of the book back to the librarian on Skellig Lir. Disinclined now to linger, Lily tucked the book into her shirt and continued along the passage in the direction of the sea. It climbed steeply for several minutes, then leveled out. At last she saw a glimmer of moonlight and heard the crashing sound of waves ahead. With eager feet, Lily hurried on to the end of the tunnel and stopped abruptly.

She was standing on the edge of a sheer fall of rock dropping down into an angry sea.

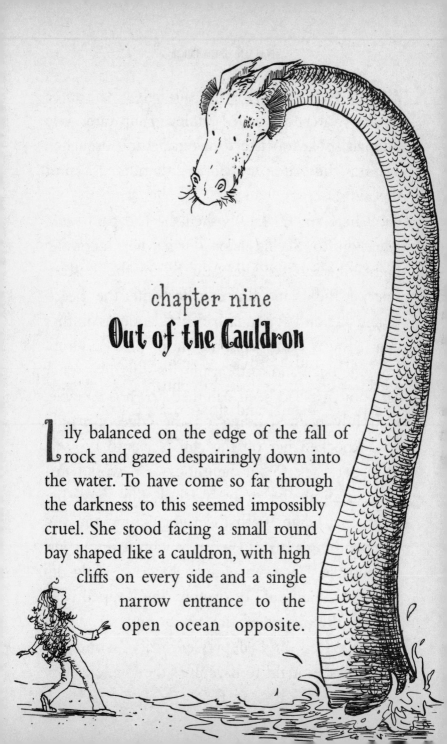

chapter nine
Out of the Cauldron

Lily balanced on the edge of the fall of
rock and gazed despairingly down into
the water. To have come so far through
the darkness to this seemed impossibly
cruel. She stood facing a small round
bay shaped like a cauldron, with high
cliffs on every side and a single
narrow entrance to the
open ocean opposite.

A huge wave came roaring through it, the force of the water channeled violently upward. Lily jumped back, too late to avoid getting drenched again as the water crashed and thundered against the cliffs.

"Where am I?" Lily wished she had paid more attention to Skellig Mor during her incoming flight. She guessed she must be on the western side of the island, directly opposite the beach where she and Romina had first landed. Another giant wave came crashing into the cauldron, slopping back and forth against its sides like water in a pot that had been slammed down on a table. Had Lily been standing on the edge, it would have knocked her off the cliff face into the sea.

To get back to the lighthouse she would first have to climb the almost vertical cliffs above her head. In daylight with the right equipment, and no incoming waves to worry about, it might just be possible. But even with night glasses, Lily did not think she could do it now. She stepped back out of the reach of the waves and sat down, feeling tired and depressed. Lily wondered whether she ought to have used the Dragons' Cry of Summoning after all. Now that Queen Dragon had left the island, it was probably too late to try.

The waves kept rolling in. After a while Lily began to notice a sort of pattern to their approach. A huge wave was followed by several big ones. But the next wave after that was usually a smaller one, and sometimes there were two little waves before the next enormous one. Interested, Lily counted five big waves, then a small one, followed by five more big ones. It looked like every sixth wave was a small one that barely wetted the cliffs.

In between waves, Lily went back to the edge and looked up at the cliff she would have to climb. Now that she had rested, it did not look quite so bad. If she timed her start just as the fifth big wave was receding, the little wave that followed should give her time to reach a narrow ledge just above the passage opening where she was standing. That would be well out of reach of even the biggest wave that might follow—or at least, Lily hoped it would be.

Lily edged over to the right-hand side of the passage opening and started counting waves. One . . . two . . . three . . . four . . . As soon as the fifth wave had broken and started its backward rush out of the bay, she pushed the toe of her left boot into a crack in the cliff face, grabbed a spur of rock with her left hand and the ledge she was aiming for with her right, and started to pull herself upward. Her right boot scrabbled against the cliff face, and when the lighthouse lamp flashed overhead, Lily quickly closed her eyes, for her night glasses made it unpleasantly bright. The sixth wave, the little one, came crashing through the entrance behind her. Lily pulled herself up a few inches on her right foot and sought for a toehold with her left. But the rock was wet and slippery, and her sodden clothes hampered her movements. Lily's left leg rubbed uselessly up and down the rock as she tried to find somewhere to put her foot, and again the light flashed and blinded her, leaving her momentarily stranded on the rock.

A great roar sounded in the cauldron: the next wave was coming. Lily made a frantic effort to plant her left foot on something firm, but the leather sole of her boot simply skidded against the cliff. Suddenly, the wave smacked against the cliff just below her and almost knocked her off.

Lily yelled, just managing to hang on by her fingertips while the water practically tore the glasses off her face.

"*Oh!*" Lily's right foot started to slither and give way. She swayed back and forth, her night glasses dangling from one ear. Without them she would be stranded in the darkness, unable to reach the top of the cliff or go back to where she'd started. Lily bent her head against her shoulder, trying to push the glasses back onto her nose, but they simply would not go on. Desperately, Lily pushed her cheek up against the cliff face right next to her hand. With the tip of one finger, she just managed to hook the night glasses over her ear.

Another wave was gathering behind her, as strong and inexorable as the last. Lily looked down through the film of water on her glasses. She glimpsed a tiny foothold in the rock and jammed her left foot into it; then, with one last surge of effort, she pulled herself up and grabbed the ledge with her right elbow. Just as she clawed her way onto it, the wave broke and splashed against the rock. This time, Lily did not care. She was beyond the reach of the water. The worst of her climb was over.

Lily clambered up the last few handholds to the top of the cliff and lay down, panting and exhausted. Inwardly, though, her spirits surged: despite everything, she had come through unhurt, except for a few small grazes. What a story to tell Queen Dragon! And there was the book she had discovered, too, to show Romina. Lily brought it out briefly from under her shirt. Its cover was a bit damp, but it had survived the worst of her drenching far better than she could have hoped.

Lily put the book away and stood up. She started walking down the hill in the direction of the beach, picking her way between rocky outcroppings and stopping at a stream for a drink of water. As she went along, she made plans about what to do next. First, she decided, she would look on the beach for some message from Queen Dragon, or an explanation as to why she had left. Then she would collect her flying cape from the rock where she had left it to dry and go in search of the mysterious Ariane.

Lily was not so sure about this idea. Her chief problem was that she was pretty sure Ariane was responsible for the ambush that had tipped her into the cavern. Lily supposed she was frightened and saw Lily as being on Romina's side; it might be hard to convince her she was a friend. But there did not seem to be any other alternative. Ariane had already attacked her once. If Lily did not find her first, she was quite likely to do it again.

Lily's feet crunched over the pebbles as she stepped onto the beach. She was so deep in thought she walked right past the rock where she had left her flying cape without even noticing. A little farther down the beach she realized what she had done and retraced her steps. But when she reached the rock, it was empty. A nasty feeling started seeping through Lily's bones, as if someone had played a trick she didn't quite know how to interpret.

Lily looked at the rock again. She was almost certain it was the one she had spread her cape over, but in case she had made a mistake she walked along the beach and checked several others without success. By now it was becoming obvious that the cape was gone. Lily started to feel panicked. In the back of her mind the flying cape had always been a sort of security: a way of returning to Skellig Lir if worst came to worst. Lily looked up at the skies, but there was not a flying cape, nor even a dragon, to be seen, only a misty banner of stars across the blackness.

The gleaming sweep of the lighthouse lamp swung around across the beach and out to sea again. It dappled the waves with light, and, as Lily followed its path, she saw something large rise up unexpectedly and plunge back into the sea again. It was a sea dragon. At the sight of it, Lily remembered why Romina had been so anxious to fix the lighthouse lamp: the sea dragons used it to guide themselves into the bay to be fed. Hundreds of sinuous shapes were swimming just off the shore, reflecting the lamplight like moving, jointed mirrors. As Lily stood watching them, a sound started creeping into her head, like a radio that was not quite on the station. It was a song, but not a human one, for it recalled to Lily's mind some of the ditties she had heard Queen

Dragon singing to herself when rooting around her metal stockpiles, or bathing in the boiling mud of her volcano crater. They were dragon nursery songs that no one could understand now except Queen Dragon herself, and the very few of her kin who still survived in the distant reaches of the world. The song she was hearing now was not the same, but Lily could see that both languages might be descended from some ancient mother tongue of dragons; and that the sea dragons had found their own remarkable way of using it.

Drawn by the music in her head, Lily walked down to the shallows and waded out into the waves. The sea dragons were coming in large numbers now, using the lighthouse lamp as a beacon, their scales shining like glass and sending little prisms of sparkling color across the water. In the midst of the throng, Lily spied a sea dragon who was bigger than all the rest. She looked old enough to be the mother of all of them, and the others seemed to defer to her, forming an escort around her as if she was someone of importance. Her eyes locked momentarily with Lily's, wild and deep and full of dreams, and then she disappeared under the waves and was seen no more.

The first sea dragons were rapidly approaching the beach. Lily had not realized how quickly they were traveling, and she turned and started wading hastily back to land. Before she could reach it, a huge wash of water rushed up unexpectedly and engulfed her; she stumbled and fell to her knees, then was knocked over sideways as the first sea dragon roared past her and beached itself, skewing around on the pebbles like a semitrailer jack-knifing on gravel. Another went past and another, nearly swamping her with their wakes. Lily reached the beach and tried to run, suddenly frightened. But by now five, ten, twelve of the creatures were blocking her path, and still they were coming ashore by the dozen, with hundreds behind them, any one of which could crush her in an instant.

"Let me pass! Please, let me pass!" Lily cried, but, of course, the sea dragons could neither hear nor understand her. They started driving along the beach toward one of the headlands that enclosed the bay, moving on tiny, hitherto unseen legs and carrying Lily with them. The stink of fish and dead marine life almost overwhelmed her. But the sea dragons somehow kept just far enough away from her to avoid crushing her to atoms, and when Lily saw an opening and put on a burst of speed, they matched her pace and hemmed her in again. In the shadow of the headland, Lily noticed a line of tanks standing near the water's edge at the end of a narrow metal gangway. The sea dragons were heading for them, and Lily suddenly guessed that these must contain the food that Ariane was supposed to give them.

The crowd of sea dragons reached the gangway. Lily tried to dodge underneath it, but immediately a sea dragon's head came crashing in beside her, ripping the metal apart like tinsel and sending her sprawling against some rocks. Lily scrambled up and screamed: another giant creature was coming at her from the other side, and she realized they were trying to drive her up onto the gangway. Lily grasped a dangling strut and pulled herself up, step by step. There was no other choice. She simply had to do what the sea dragons wanted.

Snapping and lunging, the two sea dragons

drove her along the walkway until she reached a control panel. It was as tall as Lily, with four levers protruding from its front. Lily took hold of one, gripped the hand release that was obviously meant to make the lever shift, and started pulling. There was no particular logic in what she was doing, but it seemed obvious that one of the levers *had* to operate the tanks.

But the lever refused to budge. Lily tried frantically a moment longer, then tried another, and another, and another. One of the sea dragons reared up right beside her, and she screamed, her wet boots slipping on the metal. At the same time she finally realized why she had been having so little success. The levers were interlinked and needed to be pulled together. The mechanism had been designed for an operator with four hands.

chapter ten
The Imposter

Queen Dragon flew northward, enjoying the cool pull of the night air against her leathery wings and feeling mightily satisfied with herself. Everything was resolving as she had hoped. The skies were calm, her fires were back to their normal levels, and, though she would have liked more to eat, she felt confident that she could last until landfall. The important thing was that Lily had been to Skellig Lir and discovered the secret of how to close off the Eye Stones. With that accomplished, they could head for home to work out the next step in their campaign.

Traveling on her usual perch on Queen Dragon's head, Lily was very quiet. She had not stirred much at all since leaving Skellig Mor, and, from time to time, Queen Dragon heard faint snoring sounds, as if she slept. Poor Lily, she thought tenderly. She's had a hard day. First kidnapped by that bubble, then having to pass all those tests at the Library of Skellig Lir. And learning to fly, too! That's not easy; it took me ages to get the hang of it, and I had my old mother to show me how. Of course, Lily's not a dragon; it's easy to forget that. I'm not so sure about that flying cape, either. It looks altogether too flimsy; give me a pair of stout wings, and— Queen Dragon hit a patch of turbulence, and the thought was gone. She compensated sharply. There was a cry from her head as her passenger woke up and grabbed the harness—and the unmistakable touch of a third hand.

"Lily? Is that you, Lily?" Queen Dragon demanded. There was a guilty silence that told her everything. "It's Ariane, isn't it? I might have guessed you'd try a trick like this. What have you done to Lily?"

A streak of purple light shot off Queen

Dragon's head and darted into a bank of cloud. Queen Dragon gave an exclamation of disgust and veered after it. Ariane had obviously stolen Lily's flying cape. She was a much better flier than Lily, and quicker, too. But the flying cape had its limitations, and Queen Dragon had thousands of years of experience. The most expert flier in the archipelago could not have matched her for speed or agility, especially when she was as annoyed as she was now.

Queen Dragon fixed her eyes on the purple flashes and flew up alongside them. Ariane saw her through the cloud and gave a little gasp. She tried to fly faster, but her cape was already at its limit.

"Ariane! Where is Lily?"

"Go away! I don't know where she is!"

"You do know. You must: that's Lily's cape you're wearing."

"I took it off a rock on the beach. I didn't touch Lily, I swear I didn't!"

"*Liar!*" thundered Queen Dragon. Smoke streamed out of her nostrils, and a few stray sparks shot out unintentionally with it. One caught Ariane's flying cape. The magic fabric sizzled and spat. Ariane gave a cry of alarm and flapped her arms, losing height.

"Go away!"

"Come here and get back into the harness!"

"No!" Ariane banked and flew off at an angle. Queen Dragon instantly followed, getting angrier by the moment. This chase was becoming very tedious; furthermore, as the cloud got thicker, the light from the flying cape became harder to see, and she was in danger of losing Ariane altogether. Queen Dragon dived after her into another cloud bank. Enough was enough. It was time to take drastic action.

"Ariane! Come back!"

"No!"

"All right, you little twerp. You asked for it."

Queen Dragon opened her mouth, sighted the glowing cape along her snout, and moved in like a battleship on a fishing boat. As she opened her mighty jaws, she saw Ariane glance back over her shoulder, scream, and flounder. Queen Dragon was already upon her. She lunged forward and snapped her up like a small purple fly, held her a moment in her mouth, then let her go.

"Ariane. Get back in the harness."

"Never!"

A second time, Queen Dragon moved in and lunged. Ariane buzzed about furiously inside her mouth, banging against the roof and tickling the insides of Queen Dragon's cheeks. It was a horrible sensation, and Queen Dragon had to restrain herself from swallowing. She held on as long as she could, then opened her mouth and spoke sternly as Ariane shot out.

"Give up now, Ariane. There's no point. You can't outfly me, and you can't run away from what you've done."

"No!"

Again Queen Dragon wearily snapped her up. *How many times do I have to do this?* she asked herself. Fortunately Ariane turned out to have less persistence than she had expected. The third time Queen Dragon let her go, she turned in midair, made a filthy face, and flew back to the harness with very bad grace.

"Thank you," said Queen Dragon when Ariane had strapped herself in. "Now, you and I have to have a little talk. First of all: Where is Lily?"

"I'm not telling you."

In reply, Queen Dragon wheeled in the sky

and started flapping back in the direction from which they had come. Ariane screamed. She jumped up and down in Lily's harness, and Queen Dragon could feel Ariane's tiny feet drumming furiously against her scaly head.

"No, no, no! Queen Dragon, please listen! I had to do it. I didn't want Romina to find me; she would never have let me go. Lily's perfectly safe. Please, please, please don't take me back to Skellig Mor!"

"Fat chance of that," retorted Queen Dragon. "Ariane, if you haven't figured out yet that you can't run away from problems, then it's a lesson in life you need to learn. Lily's far more important to me than you, anyway. Do you really think I'd abandon her? I'm going to ask you again, and this time I expect a sensible answer. Where is Lily?"

There was a pause, followed by a muffled reply. "In the cavern under the island."

"In the cavern? You mean the one you took me to?" Queen Dragon tried to work this scenario through. "How did Lily get in there? Did you put her in?"

"Sort of." Ariane squirmed. "Well, if you must

know, I pushed her in. Through the hole in the roof. It's quite all right. I made sure she landed in the water."

"But what if she hadn't?" Queen Dragon was appalled. "Ariane, that's terrible! What if Lily hadn't been able to swim? She could have drowned before anyone even realized she was missing!"

"But she can swim," Ariane pointed out, "so it doesn't matter, does it? And she won't be there forever. Someone will find her sooner or later and use my rope to haul her out."

"Who?" said Queen Dragon severely. "There's not a soul left on the island. Romina's already left to search for you. There's absolutely no one who would even think to look for her."

"What about the sea dragons?"

"What's Lily to the sea dragons?" snapped Queen Dragon. "You stupid girl! They'll probably eat her whole if they get a chance. And that's another thing. She'll have nothing to eat or drink in that awful place; there's not even a stream there. Oh dear, this is dreadful." The thought of Lily trapped in a dismal cavern all by herself made Queen Dragon more furious than she had been in centuries. If she had been a less responsible dragon, she would have tipped Ariane off into the ocean without a second thought.

"I don't see what you're being so touchy about," said Ariane. "I'm just calling in a favor. I rescued you off that stupid rock, didn't I?"

"Yes. Because it suited you to," said Queen Dragon. "And now it suits me to go back to Skellig Mor. Right now. This instant. And if anything's happened to Lily while we've been gone, Ariane, I promise I'll be holding you personally responsible!"

Lily stood on the metal walkway, looking despairingly at the console. There was a dinning in her head that made it nearly impossible to think. Lily tried putting her hands over her ears, but the noise was not getting into her head in the normal way, and she could not shut it out. The walkway shuddered and shook under her feet as the sea dragons threw themselves against it, growing wilder with every moment of waiting.

"Stop it! Please, stop it!" It reminded Lily of

the day the workers in the Ashby Water grommet factory had revolted. They had poured out of the factory into the scrap yard and banged their enamel plates against the factory gates, demanding more food, until the Count's Black Squads had come from the castle and driven them inside again. Like the grommeteers, the sea dragons' hunger was driving them crazy. But Lily had no idea how to stop them, or even how to tell them how helpless she was to do what they wanted.

"I've only got two hands!" she shouted. "I can't work it! *Oh!*" One of the smaller sea dragons flung itself up onto the walkway and started to slither toward her. The metal groaned and creaked under its weight. Lily lost her balance and fell hard against the console, narrowly avoiding being pitched off onto the beach.

"No! Go away!" The sea dragon's mouth opened to reveal jagged teeth, a forked blue tongue, a crusting of barnacles. Lily looked around in a panic, but there was nowhere to escape to. On one side was a beach full of sea dragons, on the other, a cliff wall that was too far to jump to and too sheer to climb. Again the fearful dinning noise surged in her head. It was coming from the sea dragons. Lily could now make out quite clearly what they were trying to say.

Eat, eat, eat. Feed, feed, feed. Eat, eat, eat . . .

"I want to help you! I want to feed you, but I don't know how!" Lily put her foot behind one of the levers and scrambled up onto the top of the console. The lever jiggled slightly as she pushed her foot down against it. Suddenly a picture flashed into her head. Lily had no idea where it had come from, but it was an image of a piece of string.

Eat, eat, eat. Feed, feed, feed. Eat, eat, eat . . . Lily turned and stared at the sea dragon on the walkway. A stink of dead fish floated toward Lily, and its mouth opened and closed like the jaws of a trap. It reminded her of the first time she had met Queen Dragon, in the scrap yard outside the grommet factory. Queen Dragon had snatched her up in her mouth and carried her away, yet she had meant no harm, and Lily had survived to become her friend. Again the picture of the length of string flashed into Lily's head, and this time she knew where it had come from. The sea dragon on the walkway had put it into her thoughts, showing her what to do.

Lily knelt down on the edge of the console and stared along the walkway at the advancing sea dragon. She concentrated, forming a picture in her head of the tank controls and her two hands resting on the levers. *Show me how,* she thought. *Show me! There has to be a way!* As Lily cast her thoughts along the walkway and across the beach, the din in her head seemed to lessen slightly. Then several things started happening all at once.

First, the sea dragon on the walkway stopped and slithered off into the crowd on the beach. As it went, a picture came into Lily's head and hung there for a second before disappearing: an image of the string tied around the top of one of the levers. Then, all the sea dragons suddenly started moving down the beach toward the water. Stones rattled like an avalanche under their scales. The sea slapped and crashed against the tanks as they tumbled into the water, and fights broke out as they struggled for the best positions.

Lily undid her boots and ripped the laces out of the eyelets. She leaned down over the controls at a perilous angle and started tying up the hand releases on the central two levers.

Eat, eat, eat. Eat, eat, eat. Eat, eat, eat . . .

"Hold on!" shouted Lily. Her fingers were clumsy with haste and dread that what she was doing was not going to work, but she could not think what else the sea dragon's picture had meant. When both releases were lashed into the open position she sat back, her bottom on the very edge of the console, and reached down with her hands for the outer two levers. Lily started pulling them upward. At the same time, she pushed down on the two central levers with her feet.

Bit by bit, the levers started to move. A grinding mechanism sounded somewhere underneath the platform, and the console shuddered furiously behind her, almost pitching her off her perch. A four-handed operator would have been facing the other way and seen exactly what was happening. But Lily could not see anything and had next to no control over what she was doing with the levers. She jammed herself back as hard as she could against the console, barely managing to stay in place.

"Come on. *Come on!*"

Slowly, the tanks behind her creaked into life.

Lily gasped with the effort of holding on. Perspiration poured down her face, and her hands started slipping on the levers. Then the line of tanks gave a great creaking thud and fell—bang, bang, bang—one after another to the right, flooding the beach with brine and writhing, twisting silver fish.

Exhausted, Lily's legs gave out. She fell with a thump onto what was left of the metal walkway and burst into sobs of relief.

chapter eleven
The Passing of the Sea Dragons

Several minutes passed before Lily was able to summon enough strength to get up. When she did, an extraordinary sight met her eyes. The sea dragons had entered a sort of feeding frenzy, tossing fish between themselves and throwing them up into the air as if enjoying some strange kind of game.

"Ugh!" An enormous, half-eaten tuna thudded onto the walkway at Lily's feet. She heaved it off with a shudder, only too glad it had not been her. The stink and the noise were awful, but, despite their unpleasant eating habits, the sea dragons no longer seemed as intimidating as they had only a few minutes before. Lily guessed that they were actually quite gentle creatures who became dangerous only when threatened or hungry or aroused to anger. Well fed, and in their own territory, they would probably be true and loyal companions.

Lily edged around the console and stood looking out over the fallen tanks at the sea dragons finishing their meal. The ones who had already fed had made room for the others and had gone back into the open bay; they were frolicking there, swimming around in circles and figure eights, their bodies intertwining and then releasing like dancers in some elaborate measure. Lily jumped down off the walkway onto the beach and walked slowly toward the water. The last of the sea dragons had gone back into the water, and those swimming in the shallows fell back as Lily approached them. Only one remained. The old mother sea dragon waited in a small pool of deep, dark water by the fallen tanks. Her liquid eyes fixed on Lily's, inky as the depths where the leviathan dwelled and old as the sea itself.

Lily knelt at the water's edge. A picture came into her mind of something spinning around in the water, something mysterious and wonderful, swirling downward. Lily saw the sea dragons swimming toward it. As she watched, a huge sea dragon came up from the depths of the whirlpool to meet them. It was snow white and bigger than all the rest, and its face was calm and beautiful. The giant sea dragon rode the swirling rapids at the top of the maelstrom, gathering in the other sea dragons like chicks under the wings of a mother hen; then it took them down safely through the whirlpool until they vanished.

"But what does it mean?" Lily asked as the picture faded. She felt desperately that she should have understood more of what she had seen. The old mother sea dragon just looked at her. Then she closed her eyes and started to turn away.

"You want to go, don't you?" The thought came to Lily from nowhere. She spoke it aloud in her head, and the little bit of dragon that was in every member of the Quench family somehow turned it into a speech that the sea dragons could understand. "Your time has come, and you want to leave. Is that what you mean?"

The mother sea dragon stopped. Suddenly Lily realized that the other sea dragons had all stopped their swimming and were listening in on the conversation. What felt like a collective sigh went up from them, as if they had finally found someone who understood.

A sense of relief and peace flooded Lily's body. She knew now what the problem was. The sea dragons were bound to the archipelago and its people. But the time had come for them to leave, and they needed the keeper's permission to go. They had asked Ariane, and she had refused them and run away. The sea dragons had felt abandoned and deeply let down. Then Lily had appeared on the beach at feeding time. They had naturally taken Lily for Ariane's replacement, and now they were asking her to give them what Ariane had refused.

Lily waded out into the water. The pale soft covering of tiny dragon scales glistened on her outstretched hand, and, when she touched the old mother sea dragon's face, the light from the tower flowed over both of them and turned her hand and the ancient creature's scales to silver.

"I understand what you're asking me," she said gently. "You may go."

Lily let her hand rest a little longer on the sea dragon's scales, then waded back out of the sea. Behind her, the sea dragons began to sing. It was like the biggest choir Lily had ever heard, a thousand voices singing in unison, but there was no sound, only an unutterable sweetness and gratitude inside her head. One by one the sea dragons sank beneath the waves, and the song became more distant and began to fade. Lily looked back. There were a thousand ripples in the still waters of the bay, and the sea dragons were gone.

Lily walked up the beach, past the ruins of the metal walkway, to a spot where a sort of path had been made up onto the headland. From its heights, she could see the sea dragons heading in their hundreds out of the cove. Lily followed them with her night glasses until they reached the straits where she and Queen Dragon had first noticed them on their flight into the archipelago. Just as they had before, they started circling. But this time, something was different. As the sea dragons swam around, the waters of the straits began to churn and swirl with them. Lily was terrified. They flowed so fast it seemed that the sea dragons must be ripped to pieces. But they were not. They simply went down into the whirlpool and vanished from sight.

The last to disappear was the old mother sea dragon. She bobbed on the edge of the maelstrom like a piece of driftwood watching the others vanish, and, at the last moment, Lily thought she saw her look back. Then she caught a glimpse of something white coming up from the depths, and the mother sea dragon went over the edge to meet it. The walls of the whirlpool came crashing in after her, and the sea dragons passed from the archipelago and out of the world. All that was left was a little foam flecking the surface of the ocean, and the first sunlight glinting on the waves.

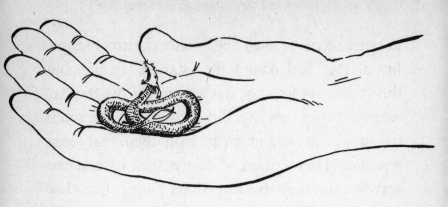

chapter twelve
The Sinking of the Cauldron

The last sea dragon had scarcely disappeared when a familiar red object appeared in the sky to the north. Lily stood watching as Queen Dragon flew down through the clouds toward Skellig Mor. As she came within range of Lily's night glasses, Lily saw that the passenger on her head was not Romina, but a stranger, a young girl with four arms whom she could only guess must be Ariane.

Lily went running back along the headland, down the path, and onto the beach. She no longer felt tired or anxious, but rather exhilarated by all that had passed. The travel, the sleepless night, the ordeals of the past few hours had simply evaporated with the dawn. She reached the beach just as Queen Dragon came into land. Another, smaller figure came flying in behind her. It was Romina, dressed in her flying cape and night glasses, returning from her search for Ariane.

"Hello, Lily!" Queen Dragon greeted her. Lily waved across the beach. She took off her night glasses, which were starting to dazzle her eyes in the dawn light, and ran toward them.

"Lily! I am so sorry," Romina said. "I just met up with Queen Dragon over the Outer Islands while I was looking for Ariane. I'd no idea what she had done, or I would never have left the island. My dear, how can I apologize?"

"There's no need," Lily assured her. She turned curiously to Ariane, who had climbed down from Queen Dragon's head and was standing a little off to one side. She was slighter than Lily, with a long tangle of silver curls and a sullen expression that no doubt owed much to having been caught. She looked to be about Lily's age, though, of course, in the archipelago, where everyone seemed to live so long, that might not necessarily mean anything.

"Ariane," said Romina sternly, "I think you have an apology to make. And something to return to Lily as well."

"I'm sorry." In Lily's opinion, Ariane did not sound very sorry. "I hope you weren't hurt when I pushed you into the cavern. This is yours. I took it off the beach." She held out a purple bundle. As it passed from her four hands to Lily's two, the folds sprang apart into a gleaming fall of fabric.

Lily gave a cry of delight. "My flying cape!"

"She wore it to trick me into believing it was you, Lily," put in Queen Dragon. "You know I never would have left you otherwise."

"Of course I do, Queen Dragon," said Lily. "But I am awfully glad to get this back. If I'd had it last night, it might have made a lot of things much easier."

Ariane gave a little sob. "I just wanted to get away from this place. I hate it here. I hate it, I hate it, I hate it!"

"Ariane, we have talked this through so many

times," said Romina wearily. "We know you are lonely. We are trying to find someone else to help you. But until we do, you'll just have to manage by yourself. The people of the archipelago need you here, on Skellig Mor. And the sea dragons need you, too."

"But the sea dragons are gone," Lily blurted out. Everyone turned to look at her.

"Gone?" asked Romina sharply. "There have always been sea dragons in the archipelago. They have lived here since the beginning of the world. How could they be gone?"

Ariane's golden face blanched pewter. "The whirlpool!" she cried. "They went into the whirlpool! Oh no!" She burst into tears and threw herself down on the shingle, sobbing as if her heart was going to break.

"How did you know?" Lily turned to her, but Ariane was crying too much to answer the question.

"They've gone! They've left me! I wasn't even here to say good-bye!"

"I don't see why you're so upset," said Queen Dragon. "*You* were quite happy to abandon *them*."

"Logic was never Ariane's strong point," said

Romina dryly. "Lily, perhaps you should explain a little further what happened."

"The sea dragons came into the beach last night to be fed," said Lily. "They seemed to think I was their new keeper. I . . . was able to understand them somehow. Maybe it's all the time I've spent with Queen Dragon, or maybe it's just part of being a Quench; I don't know. They wanted to leave the archipelago, so I told them they could go."

"You let them go!" cried Ariane. "I would never have done it. Never!"

"Poor sea dragons," said Queen Dragon warmly. "Why shouldn't they leave if they wanted to? I'm on their side. It sounds to me as if they were even more trapped here than you were, Ariane."

"I'm sorry," said Lily. She felt dreadful. "I didn't realize how important it was. I was only trying to help them."

"It is not your fault, Lily," said Romina. "Nor is it entirely Ariane's. The Drihtan and I must also take part of the blame. On several occasions Ariane tried to tell us about a huge sea dragon coming up out of a whirlpool in the straits, but we didn't believe her. We thought she was just trying to trick us into letting her off Skellig Mor." She sighed. "That aside, I am truly sorry to hear this news. The sea dragons were always our chief defense against the coming of Outsiders. Now that they are gone, we must find another way of protecting these islands, and that might not be so easy." A low whistle sounded over the water, and she looked up, shading her eyes as she looked out to sea. A boat had just rounded the headland and was setting course toward the tanks.

"Who's that?" Queen Dragon asked. "It looks like a fishing boat. Is anyone expecting visitors?"

"It's Captain Rhemus," said Romina. "He brings the sea dragons' food to Skellig Mor every morning. I'd better signal him." She walked down the beach to the water's edge and started waving her four arms in a strange and complicated semaphore. The boat changed course and started heading straight for the lighthouse. It was long and low like a yacht and painted gold so that its hull gleamed in the early morning sun. Its sails were of purple weave, shot through with flame like Lily's fireproof cape. The boat's name, *The*

Lark, was written in curling letters along the bow.

The boat sailed close to the shore, reefed in its sails, and dropped anchor. When everything was secure, a man climbed up onto the rail of the ship and launched himself into the air. His flying cape carried him across the water, and he landed a few moments later on the beach.

"Captain Rhemus!" Ariane ran over and threw her arms tightly around him. The captain lifted her up and swung her around, then set her down and gave her a hearty kiss. "Captain Rhemus— something terrible has happened! The sea dragons have left the archipelago! They've gone!"

"Gone!" The captain lifted startled eyes to Romina, who nodded sadly in confirmation. "My, my, there are strange things afoot in the archipelago this morning! A winged dragon on Skellig Mor and a stranger from the outside world. And now you tell me the sea dragons are gone. Tell me, madam—" he turned to Queen Dragon, "are you responsible? Have you driven the sea dragons out of their territory?"

"I'm afraid not," said Queen Dragon. "Pleased to meet you, Captain Rhemus. Sinhault Fierdaze, also known as Queen Dragon. This is my friend, Lily Quench."

"Miss Quench." The captain shook Lily's hand politely. "Ah, don't cry, little Ariane. It's not so bad. Just wait until you see what I've got here." He put a hand into the pocket of his flying cape. "Now, where is the little blighter? I couldn't believe my eyes when I came into the straits this morning. It was just awash with foam, and—" he pulled his hand out "—this."

Ariane shrieked aloud. "It's a sea dragon! A baby sea dragon!" The others crowded around. In the captain's hand, glistening silver-white, and opening its little mouth, was a perfect miniature of a sea dragon.

"*A* baby?" said Captain Rhemus with a joyous laugh. "You think this is it, little Ariane? There's thousands of them! They came out of the foam on the sea as we sailed in with the dawn. My sailors couldn't believe their eyes! The sea dragons must have pupped!"

"Er, I believe the correct word is 'spawned,'" said Queen Dragon, with a polite little cough, but nobody was listening. Ariane capered about like a mad thing, and Lily hugged her and then

Romina and the captain. Captain Rhemus was laughing and doing his best to stop the baby sea dragon from falling onto the beach. In the end, Queen Dragon stopped trying to explain. She sat on the shingle and looked at the baby sea dragon maternally.

"Dear little thing," she said. "And now, if you don't mind my taking the liberty, I might just eat those tanks. I'm absolutely starving." She waddled across the beach and started crunching into the metal. "Hmm. Tastes a bit fishy, but when you're as hungry as I am, a crumb's as good as a loaf of bread. Pity there isn't anything else."

"What about my cauldron?" asked Ariane, tearing herself away from the new arrival. "It doesn't seem as if I'm going to need it anymore. Romina's just said we should take the baby sea dragons back to Skellig Lir."

"Personally, I wouldn't eat it if it were the last piece of metal on earth," Queen Dragon replied. "Tow it out to sea and sink it, that's my advice."

No better suggestions were forthcoming, so while Queen Dragon finished eating, Ariane was sent off to fetch the cauldron from the cavern. By the time she came back, the morning was well advanced: a bright, clear day without a trace of cloud.

The cauldron bobbed in the waters of the bay: squat, black, and ugly. Captain Rhemus waded out and tied a silky purple rope around its lip. The rope sizzled and hissed where it touched the metal, and smoke went up as if it were on fire. The other end was made fast to a ring in the stern of *The Lark*. Then Lily, Romina, Captain Rhemus, and Ariane all went on board, and the captain whistled to the wind.

A breeze sprang up from the southwest. *The Lark*'s beautiful purple sails billowed out, and they sailed away from Skellig Mor, across the straits toward the island where Queen Dragon had cowered during the storm. When they reached a likely spot, Captain Rhemus loosed the cauldron and pulled in the rope. *The Lark* pulled away, and the cauldron spun and rocked on the peaks of the waves.

Lily climbed up onto the side of the boat so she could watch. After a few minutes Queen Dragon appeared overhead, carrying an enormous boulder in her mouth. She swooped down low over the sea and pegged the rock with unerring accuracy at the cauldron. There was a gonglike clash, followed by a gurgle as the cauldron began to founder. Then it went under, and there was nothing to be seen but a net of bubbles, prickling on the surface of the water.

"Good riddance to bad rubbish," said Queen Dragon as she flew over the boat. "Now, let's pick up those baby dragons and get back home." She banked low over the water and flew off, followed by *The Lark*, in the direction of Skellig Lir.

chapter thirteen
The Lost Book of Skellig Lir

Lily stood in the anteroom to the Library of Skellig Lir. The book she had found in the tunnel was clutched tightly in her arms, and she had just rung the bell. Its bright clear sound still hung in the air, but nobody had yet arrived to answer its summons. Lily's heart pounded, and she felt even more nervous than she had on her previous visit. If she did not get it right this time, she sensed there would be no third chance.

After a minute or two had gone by, the door slowly opened, and the librarian appeared. Her face wore a curious expression, as if she was not expecting to see Lily again so soon. Lily knelt respectfully and bowed her head.

"It's me, Lily Quench," she said. "I've found something that belongs to you. I thought you would like it back."

She held out the book uncertainly. Lily could not quite read the librarian's expression as she took it. At first, Lily thought it was one of alarm. Then she thought it was fury. Lily opened her mouth to explain that the damage was not her fault, but before the apology could leave her lips, she saw that the librarian was smiling. She closed her eyes and hugged the book to her chest, like a mother whose errant child has just come home.

"Well, Lily Quench," she said. "You've come back, and much sooner than I expected. Do you know what sort of answer you will find to your question now?"

"I think so." Ever since her first visit to the library, Lily had been putting the pieces of the puzzle together. The first clue had been the books she had seen in the Drihtan's throne room. The second had been her discovery of how the weavers made their cloth, and the third had been

Romina's mention of the Singing Wood. On the journey back to Skellig Lir, Lily had put everything together and come up with an answer. She thought she was right, but she could not be sure.

"I think," she said hesitantly, "that maybe I asked the wrong question. When I came here I expected the library to be full of books of magic spells. King Lionel and I thought that, since our problem was with something magical, we could use magic ourselves to close the Eye Stones off. But now I think that there aren't any books of magic here at all. It's the books themselves that are magical. Maybe the Library of Skellig Lir is the most magical place in all the world. I'm not sure what the answer is to my question, or even if it's here. But I should like very much to see the library all the same."

"It has taken far wiser people than you an entire lifetime to realize what you have just said to me, Lily," said the librarian. "You may have your wish. Come in."

She stepped back through the library door, and Lily felt something invisible swirl around her as she followed. She heard an impossible twitter of birds and saw a dazzle of rainbows. Then she was inside, and finally she understood what the magic of the archipelago was all about.

The library of Skellig Lir was alive.

A single great tree grew out of the bedrock of the little island. Its arching branches filled the space beneath the crystal cupola Lily had seen when she had flown over the island with Romina, and its leaves sighed and rustled in some invisible breeze. In the shelves formed by crevices in the trunk stood thousands of books, living books, that glowed with all the colors of the rainbow. A small fountain trickled down from a crystal wellhead and flowed across a carpet of soft green grass. It was filled with the same clear water Lily had seen in the Drihtan's bowl, when he showed her the books with her name on them, that had been used to keep the books alive when they were taken from the library.

A baby book was forming on a stem just above Lily's head. Its leaves fluttered and stretched like the wings of a newly emerged butterfly, and the cover changed color like ripening fruit. As Lily watched, print started appearing on the tiny pages, and miniature people in brightly colored clothes ran over the paper like insects and settled into the illustrations. All the time the book was growing bigger. When it was about the size of Lily's two hands, its leaves rustled, and the librarian came up and inspected it. She reached up her hand and grasped it, and the book came away from the tree like a piece of ripe fruit.

"Now you know why I could not let you in," the librarian said. "Imagine the damage that could be done by people who do not understand what the magic of this place is about. Human magic is nothing more than silly tricks. Real magic is about being more alive—about being closer to the way the world was when it was new." She opened the newborn book gently and laid it in Lily's hands. "Everyone who has ever been born has at least one book in this library. This one is for you, Lily. See." She pointed to the title page. With a little jolt of surprise, Lily read her name and the words, *The Lighthouse of Skellig Mor*. She turned the page to the first chapter and started reading.

High above the Southern Ocean, where the sea dragons play and the whales make their winter home, and lonely islands that the outside world has scarcely

heard of cluster, a small red speck flew steadily
southward . . .

Lily looked up and smiled. Then she read on. Time seemed to fade around her, and the sound of the birds grew faint. She did not stop reading until she reached the last chapter of the book. Only a few pages remained at this point, but around the middle of the chapter the printed words suddenly became squiggles and faded out. To her intense disappointment, Lily found she could read no further.

"What's happening? Where's the story gone?" Lily flicked quickly through to the end. The librarian took the book from her and put it on a shelf.

"That part of the story has not happened yet," she said. "It is not permitted to look into the future. Even I am not allowed to read some of the books in this library: they must stay closed until the last day of the world, when all books are opened and there will be no more secrets. But I promise you, Lily, there will be many more books of your life in the Library of Skellig Lir, and you may be certain that, when they are born,

I will take the best of care of them. I have been doing that for a very long time."

"How long, ma'am?" asked Lily shyly.

The librarian smiled. "I have been librarian here since the beginning of the world. There has never been another. And now, Lily, you had a question needing an answer. To give you that, I need to show you something. Come with me."

She led Lily around the trunk of the enormous tree. A change seemed to come over her, and her face grew stern and shadowed, until Lily felt frightened, though she did not know why. Then she saw what was wrong. On the opposite side of the tree the trunk had been split, as if by lightning. There were no shelves here, and no books, only a blackened scar where something had been violently wrenched away.

"This is where the book you found on Skellig Mor came from," said the librarian. "The Drihtan has told you about the magicians who came here long ago. This scar was made when one of them wrenched the book from the shelf and stole it. His name was Joscelin, and he had four companions with him. One of them I think you have already met. Her name was Cassandra, but you will remember her as Aunt Cassy."

"Aunt Cassy!" Suddenly lots of things started to make sense to Lily. "I met her at the Castle of Mote Ely. She knew how to operate the Eye Stones. Is that because—"

"It is because she helped to build them," said the librarian. "The knowledge of how to do it was found in the book you have just returned. It was stolen knowledge because the book was about somebody else's life, and about the future, which I have already told you is forbidden. The Eye Stones must be used carefully, Lily. Whatever you do, do not be tempted to use them to travel into your own future, for that would be perilous to everyone."

"I'd rather close them off for good," said Lily. "I thought you might be able to tell me how to do that."

"It is simple enough," said the librarian. "The Eye Stones were built using the blood of living dragons. To close them off, a dragon must let its tears fall into the Eye. When it is quite wet, the stone parts must be broken up and destroyed. But to succeed in your quest, you need to know more than I can tell you. You see, in addition to the book they stole, the magicians found and destroyed several books about their own lives. That means I cannot tell you how many Eye Stones there are, or exactly where Joscelin and the other magicians built them."

Lily was terribly discouraged. "In that case, it's no use even trying. Queen Dragon and I could close off all the Eye Stones we know about, and Gordon and his army could still come back from the past through another one."

"There may yet be a way around the problem," said the librarian. "You see, while the magicians destroyed the books about themselves, they are mentioned in other books that have continued to grow here. Look. I have put one aside for you. If you look in the front, you will see a map showing you where to find them."

Lily opened the proffered book to its frontispiece. A map was drawn there in thick black ink. It showed a place she had seen before, the strange phosphorescent river she and Queen Dragon had flown over on her way to the Singing Wood. Suddenly Lily seemed to fall forward into the map. The dark lines stretched away before her and she followed the river, and then its tributaries, into the distant north. The desert sands gave way to rocky country and a mountain range, and then to a weird sedgy landscape filled with dozens of small pyramids drawn in thick black strokes. A small figure in a black robe was standing at the foot of the largest one. It was a man and, to Lily's horror, he looked up, as if trying to see her. She shuddered, and then all at once the page was small again and the librarian was reaching for the book to put it away.

"I see you have found some answers, Lily," said a familiar voice. Lily turned and saw that the Drihtan and Romina had entered the library behind her.

"I think so," she said. "At any rate, I am very glad that I came."

"Then your visit has been worthwhile for you as well as us," said the Drihtan. "Lily, it is time for you to leave us. But, before you go, I must give you some gifts. First, your fireproof cape has been mended for you and washed in moon rose water to strengthen its weave. With care, it should last your family another hundred and fifty years. The flying cape you wore to Skellig Mor is yours to take as well, a present from the weavers to the Quench family. And finally, here is a gift from the people of the archipelago, in gratitude for the return of our missing treasure."

The Drihtan handed Lily a small box made of mother-of-pearl. She ran her fingers gently over it. A soft click sounded somewhere inside, and a waft of sweet perfume filled the air. A concealed lid sprang open to reveal a single moon rose, carefully dried and preserved without a petal out of place.

"The moon rose trees cannot grow in the lands beyond the archipelago," said the Drihtan, "or I would give you a cutting to plant. But it would perish in the outside world, and so, instead, I offer you this piece of advice. Whenever you are feeling sad or downhearted, Lily, open the box and smell the moon rose. Let its scent remind you of the way things were when the world was new and unspoiled, and you will be able to look at everything afresh."

"Thank you," said Lily simply. "I will treasure it always." She turned to the librarian and curtsied. "Good-bye," she said, "and thank you.

I have learned so much today, I do not think I will ever be able to repay you."

"To be grateful is often the hardest lesson of all," said the librarian. "Good-bye, Lily. Good luck and safe journeying."

She lifted her hand in farewell. Then she faded, and the library with her, and Lily was standing alone in the courtyard outside the Drihtan's palace. The sun was shining on the golden island in the center of the pavement, and she could hear a swallow twittering as it winged its way to its nest.

The moon roses were in blossom as Lily walked away from the Drihtan's palace and headed off to meet Queen Dragon. There was no sign of any damage from the storm. In the moon rose orchards young men and women were spreading sheets on the ground under the trees to catch the falling blossoms. They stopped as Lily passed, and bowed politely before returning to their work.

Lily walked on beneath the trees, breathing in their scent and marveling again at how beautiful everything was here. A gentle breeze was blowing, and the blossoms fell like rain on her hair and cheeks. It seemed no wonder that the people of Skellig Lir lived so long, when the air smelled like this. Lily passed beneath the last of the trees and walked down a gentle slope to a sandy beach. Queen Dragon was sitting on the shore with Ariane, watching the baby sea dragons play in the special shallow pool that had been set aside for them.

"Poor little orphans," Queen Dragon sighed as Lily walked up. Her eyes were positively misty. "No mother to look after them. It's a tragedy."

"They're not orphans," said Ariane indignantly. "They've got me."

"You haven't been much help so far," said Queen Dragon severely. "You weren't even there when they were born."

"Don't rub it in, Queen Dragon," said Lily. "I'm sure Ariane will be a wonderful mother, and there'll be lots of people to help her."

"Well, she's certainly got her work cut out for her," said Queen Dragon. She got up and waddled across the grass. Lily said good-bye to Ariane and followed her. When they reached an open space that was suitable for take-off, she slung her pack down onto the ground and took out the two magical capes to show Queen Dragon.

"Look. They've given me the flying cape I wore to Skellig Mor. Should I wear it now, or Mad Brian Quench's fireproof one?"

"The fireproof one," said Queen Dragon firmly. "I'm sorry, Lily, but my wings are much more efficient than that cape thing. Especially over long distances."

"I suppose so," said Lily wistfully. "It was awfully fun, though. I'd always wondered what it would be like to fly."

"Keep it for special occasions then," said Queen Dragon. "Like your birthday, or the Royal Christmas Party."

"I could take off during King Lionel's Christmas Message. Just imagine it!" Lily paused, then regretfully shook her head. "I'd never do it, of course. It wouldn't be fair. But it would . . . it would be awfully funny, wouldn't it?"

"Yes, it would." Queen Dragon made a most undragon-like noise, somewhere between a giggle and a snort. "Back to Ashby, then?"

"To Ashby," Lily agreed, and she climbed up the scaly ridge on Queen Dragon's neck to her accustomed seat. As she buckled her flying cape and moon rose box onto the luggage harness, the conversation she'd had with King Lionel on the eve of their departure came back to her. "It will be hard for you, of course," Lionel had said. "But then, it always is. Until we can close off the Eye Stones, Ashby and everything we have fought for will be at risk. We take the good times for granted and think the bad times will never come back. But that isn't true. It's not one battle, Lily, but an ongoing fight that will never go away and never finish while we have breath in our bodies or hope in our hearts."

"Home to Ashby," repeated Lily. "And then to the Magicians' Pyramid."

Don't miss these other
exciting adventures. . . .

Lily Quench and the Dragon of Ashby

As a family of dragon slayers, the Quenches of Ashby have always been burning successes... until the evil Black Count invades, and the family's fortunes go into a downward spiral.

Then a dragon unexpectedly arrives, and Lily, the last of the Quenches, is called upon to fight it. Soon she finds herself on a desperate, magical quest to save Ashby from destruction—and restore the lost heir to his throne. . . .

Join Lily on a perilous mission. . . .

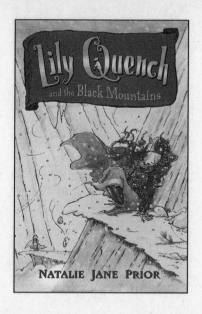

Lily Quench
and the Black Mountains

NATALIE JANE PRIOR

Lily Quench and the Black Mountains

In the Black Mountains there's nothing but snow and ice. But it's there that the magical blue lily grows, which can help Lily Quench stop the evil Black Count from invading her homeland.

With her friend Queen Dragon, Lily embarks on a perilous mission to bring the blue lily back to Ashby. Captured and imprisoned, then befriended by the count's son, Gordon, they flee to the eerie heights of Dragon's Downfall . . . the place where Lily and Queen Dragon must confront their greatest fear.

Lily Quench and the Treasure of Mote Ely

Kidnapped and taken back into the past to a crumbling castle in the middle of a creepy marsh, Lily Quench searches for the long-lost treasure of Mote Ely—and a way back to her own time.

Locked in a dungeon, attacked by a dragon, and befriended by her eccentric great-great-great-great grandmother, Lily finds that enemies can sometimes be friends—and that old friends can unexpectedly turn into enemies.